TAINTED TOWNS

Three Sinister Suburban Tales

VICTORIA WILLIAMSON

Silver Thistle
Press

This edition published By Silver Thistle Press Ltd in 2025

Silver Thistle Press Ltd
272 Bath Street,
Glasgow
G2 4JR

For all enquiries, please email: enquiries@silverthistlepress.com
www.silverthistlepress.com

978-1-7384364-7-7

Printed in Great Britain

This book is dedicated to all those from small towns who have seen shadows dance outside their cosy living-room curtains, heard what the wind whispers to the nightbirds nesting in their carefully pruned hedges, and imagined more sinister things lurking in dark suburban streets than the comforting monotony of daily life might suggest.

Tunnel Vision

The first time the shadow followed her down the tunnel, Helen thought she was simply imagining it.

The underpass was badly lit, after all, and as a single woman making her way home at eight o'clock on a dark winter night, she was bound to be jumpy, especially as she wasn't familiar with the neighhour-hood yet. It must have been her overactive imagination playing tricks on her.

Yes. That's all it was.

Nothing more.

Everything else about her move to the city had gone well – as well as it could possibly have gone after such a messy and heart-wrenching breakup, that is. Just six weeks ago, Helen had her whole life planned out. She lived in the same small town where she'd grown up, met regularly with her old school friends for coffee and a gossip, and was engaged to her childhood sweetheart. The house they lived in wasn't large, but the old-fashioned wood panelling had a rustic charm, and the garden was full of wild roses in summer. On her days off from the local library where she enjoyed keeping the shelves in order and chatting to the regulars about books at the reception desk, Helen's home project had been shaping up nicely. She'd already finished painting the spare bedroom in pretty pastel colours in the hopes that it would one day become a nursery after her wedding that Christmas, and had made a start on taming the wild garden by pulling up two of the sprawling hydrangea bushes to make way for the swing set she intended to buy for her future children.

She'd just finished drawing up the seating plan for the wedding, when she'd found out her fiancé had been having an affair with her best friend for the last two years.

The worst thing was: everyone had known about it for ages. *Everyone.*

Her mother had wrung her hands and told Helen she hadn't wanted to rock the boat, especially as Kevin was such a nice man with such a steady job at the bank. Her father had patted her on the shoulder and assured her it was just a phase Kevin was going through – he was still young after all, and all young men strayed from time to time, didn't they? Her sister had shrugged and said it wasn't the first time Kevin had cheated on her since they'd started dating at fourteen, so there was no point making a fuss now they were engaged. And Helen's group of friends had made various excuses, ranging from it 'not being their place' to interfere in her relationship, to 'not wanting to take sides'. Worst of all, her best friend Meg had refused to discuss the subject, saying that Helen needed to work things out with Kevin herself.

If only Kevin had made some show of contrition, had at least *looked* like he was ashamed of his behaviour, then Helen would have been able to keep up the pretence that their relationship wasn't a complete sham. If he'd just played the part of a repentant sinner who'd seen the error of his ways, then Helen could have shone in her role as the wronged but forgiving girlfriend, hiding behind a mask of saintly forbearance to escape the sting of public humiliation.

But Kevin refused to play his part. He didn't see anything wrong in having his bit on the side – he was marrying her and paying the mortgage and most of the bills, wasn't he? What more did she want?

It was the realisation that she'd be serving as the unwilling third wheel in an open marriage shared not just with strangers, but with women she'd thought of as her closest and most trusted friends, that finally forced Helen to cancel the wedding.

She couldn't stay in her home town after that. It was too small, and everyone knew about the affair. She couldn't face the looks of pity and the awkward words of condolence from the regulars across the library counter. She couldn't stand the whispers at church and the way her face burned with shame when the minister talked of adultery, feeling as though every word was directed at her despite her being the injured party. She couldn't bear the knowing looks her parents shot each other when she stayed with them while she worked out what on earth to do. And she couldn't trust her childhood friends, not after she'd discovered the enormity of the secret they'd been colluding to hide from her.

Escaping from Kevin and his indifference was the most pressing reason for moving to the city, though. Neither of them had done well at school, but she'd worked hard to support Kevin through many years of further education, tempering her disappointment at his endless exam resists with the comforting thought that she was investing in their future life together. It took him seven years to complete his university degree in accountancy, but when he'd finally gained a well-paid job as manager of their local bank that summer, her plans seemed to be bearing fruit at last. She'd ditched her stressful work at the call centre and her evening shifts at the supermarket checkout, finding a wonderful part-time job at the library while pursing her dream of writing a children's book. That dream had lasted for exactly two months, and then she'd found out about the affair.

She had to move. The whole house was full of memories of the imagined life that was no longer within her grasp.

In more practical terms, it was full of *Kevin*, and as she'd naively allowed him to take out the mortgage in his name all those years ago in anticipation of his future bread-winning role, he insisted the house was rightfully his. She didn't have the strength or the finances to fight him. She could either stay and put up with his behaviour, or move out.

Helen moved out.

She moved as far as she could, feeling as though her heart was splitting in two and the future she'd planned was sliding further from reach with each mile she travelled on the long-distance bus. There were two versions of her life now. There was the dream she'd toiled for years to achieve – the dream in which Kevin was a doting and dutiful husband, coming home from the bank each evening to the dinner she cooked for him and their brood of adorable children. And then there was her new reality. A pokey apartment on the twelfth floor of a high-rise at the edge of a distant city, and a job at the reception desk of a large chain hotel where hundreds of guests passed through each day as they travelled to and from the airport.

The last two weeks of her new life hadn't been *bad* exactly. Just different. A different set of apartment rooms she was not yet familiar with despite their claustrophobic dimensions. A different parade of visitors past her reception desk at work, all transitory and too engrossed in their travel plans to engage with her attempts at small talk. A different set of colleagues, none familiar, and none interested in discovering the details of her life or disclosing theirs.

And then there was the walk home when her shift ended at eight each evening.

That was the only part of her new life she struggled to imagine adapting to.

The pedestrian underpass crossed beneath the motorway that connected the outskirts of the city to the airport and the world beyond. It was reached by a long flight of stone steps at the far end of the hotel car park, in a dark corner the dim streetlights never quite seemed to reach. Its damp walls were adorned with black and white tiles arranged in abstract shapes that might once have been considered the height of brutalist chic, but which were now dingy and depressing, stained by decades of graffiti and urine and stinking of neglect. There were six old fluorescent strips set into the roof at intervals calculated to provide the bare minimum of light to meet safety requirements as well as the council's meagre budget. The four in the centre of the underpass looked like they hadn't worked in years. The one at the entrance buzzed loudly in warning of its imminent failure, while the other at the far end was temperamental, sometimes deigning to provide illumination, but often fading in despondence at the lack of attention paid to its state of disrepair.

The first time Helen walked down that tunnel at the end of her hotel shift, the hair on the back of her neck had stood on end the whole way.

It wasn't just its isolated position connecting a faceless hotel to the neglected high-rise buildings at the scrag end of the city that created such an air of desolation around it. And it wasn't just the gloomy lighting that produced a sense of danger and dread when Helen approached the dark mouth at the base of the steps. There was something strange about that tunnel, some ineffable atmosphere that seeped through the walls and clung to Helen as she hurried down the long passage, holding her breath the whole way until she was safely on the other side.

When she mentioned the unpleasant experience to various coworkers the next day, she was met with indifference. The shift manager had a car and drove to work. The two other receptionists took the bus home from the hotel stop. The restaurant staff were too busy to chat despite her attempts to get their attention, and the three cleaners she tried to strike up conversation with during her break didn't speak English.

Her sense of isolation only deepened over the next two weeks, each short walk back to her twelfth-floor apartment forcing her to run the gauntlet of the underpass at the end of each shift. She never met another living soul on the lonely walk down that stagnant tunnel, not until the thirteenth night.

That was when she saw the shadow for the first time.

Helen was halfway through the underpass, when she was hit by the unpleasant feeling that someone was behind her. A cold shiver ran down her spine, one hand automatically curling into a protective fist while the other gripped her purse strap tighter. Despite her sudden fear, habitual social inhibition stopped her from turning to look behind, at least at first. What if no one was there? She'd look a nervous fool, even if there was no one to judge her actions but herself. And what if there *was* someone behind her? What if it was a *man*? That would be worse. Then her mind would spiral in panic as it tried to work out whether to break into a run and risk looking like a mad woman if he turned out to be a perfectly ordinary pedestrian, or whether to continue at the same pace and risk life, limb, or the loss of her purse.

Her mind froze under the deluge of conflicting impulses.

Run. *Walk.*

Don't take the risk. *Don't look stupid.*

Stare straight ahead. *Look behind.*

Look behind look behind look behind!

The final thought proved the strongest, the urge to

turn her head too powerful to resist. Right up until the last moment, she'd been almost sure the sensation of being followed was just her overwrought mind playing tricks on her. But then she turned around and saw it.

It.

There was no other word to describe the dark shape in the tunnel behind her. Silhouetted against the orange glow at the mouth of the underpass, an indistinct blur was moving swiftly and surely towards her. She could feel malevolent intent emanating from the shadow, a desire to reach her, to...

Helen didn't wait to find out what that sinister shape in the dark wanted.

Tearing her gaze from the terrible sight of the figure bearing down on her, she raced for the underpass exit, the heels of her uncomfortable work shoes clicking on the concrete. It wasn't a long distance, but it felt like a mile. Her lungs were burning with the effort of sucking air down a throat constricted in panic by the time she burst from the tunnel mouth and ran up the ramp to the street surrounding the high-rise buildings. Forced to stop to let a car pass on the narrow road, she glanced back, her heart pounding at the thought of what might emerge from the underpass.

The mouth of the tunnel yawned emptily in the brighter light from the housing estate streetlamps.

It's waiting, she thought to herself as she tripped across the road in her ill-fitting heels and headed for her apartment building. *It's in there and it's waiting for me.*

What *it* was, and what *it* wanted, she couldn't begin to imagine.

By the time she reached the building at the far end of the estate and rode the elevator to the twelfth floor, Helen had started to question whether it wasn't her imagination that had been the problem after all. She'd had such a rough couple of months. So much upheaval. So many changes. Such a lot on her mind.

Perhaps she was just tired. Perhaps all she needed was some hot food, a warm shower, and an early night.

That might be what she needed, but what she desperately wanted was some human contact. Back home, in her snug house with wood panelling and wild roses in the garden, she'd had Kevin's warm, if slightly flabby body to curl up next to on the sofa in the evening. If he was working late, she could visit her parents just three streets away, drop in on her neighbours for a chat, or call some of her friends over for wine, pizza and a movie. She'd had options, back then. So many of them. She could do none of that now.

She hung her winter coat up on the single hook in the narrow hallway and gazed around her tiny apartment. Despite doing her best to give it some homely touches – a crochet blanket on the back of the couch, a hand-painted sunset in the frame on the wall – it seemed to have all the charm and warmth of a dentist's waiting room. This was just a rented set of rooms. It wasn't her house. It wasn't home.

Home.

At the thought of all she'd left behind, Helen felt the familiar tearing sensation in her chest, as though the two halves of her broken heart were pulling at the sutures where she'd tried to stitch them together. She couldn't pretend she was fine with the way her life had turned out. Not tonight.

Picking up the phone, she dialled her parents' number. She'd called them briefly when she'd first arrived to let them know she was safely at her destination, but she'd asked them not to ring her while she settled in and adjusted to her new life. She couldn't bear to hear the disappointment in her mother's voice and the loud sighs of disapproval from her father in the background.

Now, even sounds of disappointment and disapproval from home would be better than the heavy silence of the unfamiliar apartment.

"Hello, Mum. Just thought I'd call to catch up. You're not busy just now, are you?" Helen knew her mother liked to bake in the evenings. The kitchen, with its trays full of buns and pots of freshly made soup was her refuge from the chaotic noise of the living room where Helen's unemployed father sat watching TV all day. Helen knew it wasn't his fault that jobs were scarce and his education was too patchy for him to retrain at this late stage, but the unedifying example of her parents' marriage gave her yet more cause to regret leaving the safety of her relationship with a man of solid education and financial substance.

"Helen! Finally! I was getting worried. Jerry, it's Helen." Her mother shouted this last remark over the blaring television in the background. Helen didn't hear her father's reply, but the ear-splitting volume of the comedy show was lowered just enough to prove her father wasn't completely indifferent to her despite her disappointing choices. "That's better," her mother sighed. "Now, Helen, have you spoken to Kevin?"

Helen's heart sank. She should have known that would be the first thing her mother would ask despite all the other big changes in her life.

"No, Mum. It's all over with Kevin. There's no reason for me to speak to him now." She tried to keep the irritation from her voice, reminding herself that Kevin had been a big part of her parents' lives too ever since she'd introduced him to them nearly fifteen years ago. "Things are going well here," she said, affecting a cheery tone to signal the change of subject. "I've settled in to the apartment, and my job's been an interesting change from—"

"But Helen, pet," her mother interrupted, fixed on the one subject Helen had hoped to avoid, "you can't ignore Kevin forever. He really is sorry, you know. I saw him at the supermarket the day after you left, and he looked so lonely shopping for microwave meals for one, I had to ask him to dinner. He misses you so much. He was telling me on Tuesday that he isn't going to sell the house, he's going to keep everything just the way you left it, in case you change your mind. And last night he said—"

"*Mum*!" Helen cried. "How many times have you had Kevin over for dinner since I left?"

"Only a few times, pet. Maybe two or three. Something like that. How many times has Kevin been to dinner, Jerry?" she asked, seeking backup from her husband. "It's just been a couple of nights, hasn't it?"

Over the din of the TV in the background, Helen clearly heard her father shout, "Ten!" His voice was annoyingly triumphant.

"Yes, two," her mother said over the phone, unaware that Helen had heard the reply. "I know he's not quite our son as you two haven't married yet—"

"—And never will—"

"—but he's the closest thing we've got," her mother continued as if Helen hadn't spoken. "Will you not call him, Helen? If you say you're sorry, I know he'd take you back in a heartbeat. Then things can go back to the way they were before all this nonsense."

"Say *I'm* sorry?" Helen spluttered. "*He's* the one who cheated on *me!*"

"But that's all in the past now!" her mother insisted. "He won't do it again. One little phone call, that's all it would take to clear up the misunderstanding, I know it is. Will you not, Helen?"

Helen passed a hand across her eyes. They ached from long hours spent staring at hotel reservations and customer requirements on a computer screen. She felt weary to her bones, but it wasn't just work that exhausted her. Managing her parents' unrealistic expectations was even harder than dealing with demanding hotel guests at work.

"Look, I've got to go, but I just wanted to let you know everything's alright here. I'll speak to you next week, OK?"

"OK, pet. I hope you can work things out soon." Her mother managed to pack a lifetime's worth of disappointment into that short line before she put the phone down.

Helen slumped onto the couch, too tired now to consider making anything more strenuous than a microwave meal for dinner. She should've anticipated exactly how that conversation would go. What was she thinking, calling her mother for emotional support she knew would never be forthcoming? Her parents wanted her to be happy, but their version of happiness required feigning ignorance of the fact that her former fiancé was a two-timing rat. Helen was sick of pretending. Even the effort of five minutes of fake cheerfulness on the phone to her mother was more than she could bear.

With no one else she could call who wouldn't make everything about Kevin and the mistake they thought she'd made in leaving him, Helen opted for a few hours of television to take her mind off the unsettling experience in the underpass.

It wasn't until she woke at 3 a.m. with a stiff neck and her cheek squashed against the arm of the couch that she realised she'd dozed off in front of the TV without even eating the curry she'd left congealing in the microwave. She switched the TV off and climbed into bed, but sleep no longer wanted to befriend her. Left alone with her thoughts, she stared at the ceiling until morning, trying not to dwell on the fact that the light dawning behind the curtains left a bright patch not unlike the glow of streetlights at the end of the underpass, or that the bird sitting on the windowsill outside cast an eerily similar shadow to the one she'd seen following her the night before.

By the time her hotel shift started, Helen was almost glad of the excuse to be around other people again. The walk to work was so different to the one she'd had the night before. In the cold light of day, there was nothing particularly odd about the underpass. It was just a dreary concrete tunnel, no more remarkable than the thousands of other ugly constructs that blighted cityscapes across the country. There were no moving shadows, just the long gloom of a winter morning. Even the strange atmosphere seemed to have dissipated in the indifferent sunlight that struggled through the grey clouds.

The day was so ordinary, so numbingly mundane, that by the end of her shift, Helen had almost forgotten the fright she'd had the night before. It was only when she'd collected her coat from the staffroom and had stepped from the warm lobby into the cold car park, that she remembered she'd have to pass down the dark tunnel to return to her apartment.

Helen's pace slowed as she reached the end of the car park, and she hesitated at the top of the steps leading down to the underpass. She gazed back, checking to make sure there was no one who would be following behind her. A car door slammed, and she waited for its owner to retrieve his case from the back seat and trundle it into the hotel. A bus drew up at the front entrance, disgorging passengers into the frosty gloom and picking up a group of tired cleaners who had finished the day shift. Still Helen waited, watching as the passengers made their way into the hotel and the bus drove off with its new consignment of dead-eyed commuters.

On the motorway above the tunnel, cars roared past behind steel railings, their headlights dazzling in the dark. There was no one else in sight. Helen was alone.

Finally satisfied there would be no repeat of the night before, Helen hurried down the stairs, determined to get back to the apartment as fast as she could and make a proper dinner this evening. Perhaps she'd make a pot of soup, or a chicken casserole with—

Oh.

There it was again.

That feeling.

The horrible, hair-raising sensation that someone, *something*, was behind her.

Helen quickened her pace, wishing she'd thought to bring a change of shoes to work. The click of her heels echoed through the strangely silent tunnel that seemed impervious to all sound from the world outside, emphasising how vulnerable she was. The orange glow at the far end of the underpass seemed further away now than when she'd entered, the distance stretching paradoxically in her mind's eye as the pauses between her heartbeats shortened, until her chest felt like a drum pounding non-stop in warning.

Don't look back.

Don't look back.

Don't look back.

Helen looked back.

The shadow was moving swiftly down the tunnel towards her, the sense of malevolent intent radiating from its indistinct form even stronger this time. The darkness seemed to pulsate in a way that was both disturbing and disorientating, as though the nebulous shape hazily outlined against the orange glow of the tunnel entrance was both very much there, yet at the same time, not there at all.

Helen stifled the urge to scream, saving her breath for the sprint to the exit. The hair on the back of her neck prickled so sharply in warning it was almost painful, but she couldn't risk looking back again to see if the thing had caught up with her. All she could do was charge for the entrance, praying her heels wouldn't break as they slammed painfully against the hard concrete.

Bursting out of the underpass, this time Helen didn't stop until she reached the safety of the first tower block at the edge of the estate. When she finally turned and peered across the road, she could see nothing in the darkness of the underpass at the bottom of the ramp. The temperamental sixth light was off, hiding whatever might be lurking just inside the tunnel mouth.

I should call the police, Helen thought. *There's something in there that enjoys chasing women at night.*

Some*thing*. Not some*one*. How was she supposed to explain that without sounding crazy? They'd question if she was overworked, overwrought. As soon as she mentioned her recent breakup and relocation to an unfamiliar city, they'd put her strange sightings down to stress. No, it was better for her to simply buy a torch and a rape alarm, and trust the combination of light and sound would scare away anything lurking in that tunnel. Tomorrow was Sunday. She had the day off to rest. And to shop.

She ignored the nagging voice at the back of her head that kept asking what use gadgets would be against something that wasn't quite human. Now that she was back in the more solid world beyond the liminal space of the tunnel that distorted her sense of reality, she refused to believe it wasn't a man who'd been chasing her. It was some creep who got off on scaring woman, that's what it must be. And with her torch and wailing rape alarm, next time he tried anything, she'd be ready.

Pulling herself together, Helen managed to force down an unappetising microwave meal *before* she gave in to the urge to pick up the phone and call home. It wasn't her mother she called. Tonight, she tried to find the comfort she was seeking from her former close friend,

Tracey.

"Hi, Trace, it's Helen. How's things?" Helen tried to keep her voice upbeat. The happier she sounded, the less the likelihood that Tracey would suspect she was being eaten up by regret. Her fake enthusiasm for her new life should steer the conversation firmly away from the past and the painful topic of Kevin.

"Oh... Hi, Helen. I wasn't expecting you to call." Her tone wasn't quite accusatory, but there was an edge of unease in Tracey's voice.

"Sorry – is this a bad time?" Helen bit her tongue as soon as she said it. She'd spent so much of her life worrying about upsetting people, putting people out, letting people down, that apologising for her existence had become almost second nature. That was a habit she'd have to break now that she'd moved away.

New life. New Helen Bates.

"No, I just… Hold on, I'll go into the other room."

Helen heard a few hushed words being exchanged and the clink of a wine glass being set on a kitchen counter. It was only a few seconds of sound in the background, but it was more than enough for her to picture the scene and to identify the actors on stage.

"Tracey, is that Kevin who's there with you?"

"No! Well… Yes, it is actually, but it's not what you think!"

Helen heard the sound of a door closing and Tracey's footsteps padding down the hallway's wooden floorboards to the living room.

"I see. And what exactly *is* Kevin doing at your apartment, Trace?" Helen fought to keep the sourness from her tongue as bile rose in her throat at the thought of her ex-fiancé taking up with yet another of her friends behind her back.

"He just came over to return the rice cooker – you know, the one you borrowed for the barbecue you held in the summer?"

"Oh."

Helen wasn't sure now what to think. She *had* borrowed the rice cooker to make sure there would be enough food for the vegetarians in the group that evening. She *had* been promising Tracey for months that she'd return it. And then in the chaos following her breakup with Kevin, she *had* forgotten all about it.

But still…

The nagging little voice in her head had returned, this time whispering that she was a fool if she trusted Tracey any more than she'd trusted her former best friend, Meg.

Shut up, she told the voice. *Maybe Mum's right, maybe Kevin is just lonely and looking for people to talk to. We all went to school together – he knows my friends almost as well as I do.*

And he knows some of them much better than you do, the voice said nastily.

"Well, I just called to let you know I'm settling in fine," Helen said loudly to drown out the words she didn't want to hear. "Work's going really well, and I love my snug little apartment. You should come and visit some time, we'll have a lot of fun – there's loads to do here in the city."

Helen's cheerfulness sounded forced, even to her own ear. She knew Tracey was going to pass everything on to Kevin as soon as she hung up, and desperately wanted him to know how much better her life was without him, even if it wasn't true.

"That's great, Helen. Once the weather's better I'll definitely make the trip over. It'd be great to do some sight-seeing with you." Tracey's enthusiasm sounded every bit as fake as Helen's cheerfulness did.

Helen decided to call it quits.

"OK, well, I'm going out with some workmates tonight, so I'll speak to you soon, alright?" Helen bit her tongue to avoid adding any messages of greeting for Kevin. The lie about her non-existent social life was a clumsy enough blunder for one night.

"Sounds good. Bye, Helen."

"Bye."

This time when Helen hung up, she felt not just lonely, but sick. It was bad enough her parents were acting as if nothing had changed by inviting Kevin to take her place at their dinner table. Now, it seemed, her friends had barely noticed her absence, and were carrying on as if she'd never existed. She was stuck in this dreary apartment in a faceless city doing a job she couldn't care less about, while Kevin continued his life in the house with the wood panelling and wild roses, welcomed with open arms by her friends and family as though *she* was the one who'd been exiled for cheating.

How was that fair?

He's not worth it, forget about him, she told herself, turning the TV on as loud as her neighbours would tolerate to drown out the nasty little voice in her head that spoke the truth over the lies she preferred. Hugging a cushion to her chest, she tried to hold the two halves of her broken heart together, feeling again the disorienting sensation of living two different lives at once – the one of her dreams, and this nightmare she couldn't wake from.

Her dreams that night were troubled, filled with darkness and shadows, and an eerie clicking that sounded like the countdown of a fateful clock.

Rising early, determined to shake off her fears, she spent the next day in the city, browsing the shops and pretending she enjoyed her new life unencumbered by a fiancé, friends or family. She wandered around the modern art gallery, trying not to hear Kevin's voice sneering in her head that a chimp could paint better than most of the so-called masters on display. She visited fancy stores too exclusive to display their prices, trying not to hear her mother sighing that she'd never afford anything nice again after leaving her banker boyfriend. She passed women in the mall locked in conversation and giggling over coffee, trying not to think of the friends she'd lost and the shared history she'd no longer revisit. She ate a late lunch on her own in a bookshop café, pretending to write story ideas in a notebook so strangers would mistake her for the author she'd always wanted to be. By the time she'd bought a rape alarm, a torch and a pair of running shoes she could slip on after work, she felt so lonely she wanted to cry.

Too dispirited by the thought of a solo dinner and a theatre seat for one, she took the bus back to her apartment when it got dark, watching the bright lights of the city give way to the dreary orange glow of the council estates as the bus carried her to the outskirts of civilisation. At least it set her down on the high-rise end of the underpass rather than outside the hotel. Escaping the walk through the underpass after such a dismal day was one small mercy.

Her evening routine was exactly the same as every other night since she'd arrived: a microwave meal; a movie or two until she fell asleep on the couch; an uncomfortable waking in the middle of the night; a move to her bed; then a few hours of fitful rest until her alarm clock went off.

Rinse, repeat.

This was her life now. There was no point in fighting against it.

What she could fight, though, was the thing in the underpass. She wasn't exactly looking forward to seeing it again, but after buying the rape alarm, all next day at work she felt a frisson of anticipation at the thought of the loud noise scaring it away. It would be one small victory to combat the nagging feeling of failure that had dogged her since leaving home.

Standing at the top of the steps at the end of her shift, staring down at the tunnel entrance and wondering how far she'd get before the fear gripped her, her new-found confidence evaporated.

Get a grip, she ordered herself. *You have a torch and a rape alarm, and you've got sensible shoes on. You can scare off whatever's down there. And if you can't, you can always outrun it.*

Her new running shoes pinched her toes, and the bag with her work heels thumped awkwardly against her thigh as she hurried down the steps. Even with a torch in one hand and the rape alarm clutched tightly in the other, she didn't feel prepared to face the thing that pulsed with malevolent intent in the dark.

Tonight, though, she had a plan. She wasn't going to turn round. No matter how painfully the hair on the back of her neck prickled, no matter how overwhelming the urge to turn her head, she wasn't going to look over her shoulder, she wasn't going to give in.

She was simply going to set her alarm off, and run.

And that's exactly what she did.

The second she felt the terrible sensation that something was approaching, she pressed the button on her alarm and took off down the tunnel.

It didn't go to plan.

There was something wrong with the alarm. There must be – why else would the shrill sound she'd been expecting to hear fade to a low moan as though it was being swallowed by the hungry tunnel walls? Why else would her pounding heart sound louder than the thump of sensible shoes on concrete?

Her torch seemed to be malfunctioning too. No matter how hard she pressed the switch, the dazzling light she'd seen in the hardware store was now no brighter than a match. That forlorn light was worse than total darkness, for in the feeble glow new shadows multiplied on the walls until she couldn't tell if the thing she was escaping was behind or in front of her.

Worst of all, there was something wrong with her new shoes. How else could she explain the fact that no matter how hard she swung her legs and arms, she couldn't seem to run any faster than when she'd been wearing heels?

Turn around turn around turn around, her voice was screaming in her head.

But she wouldn't. Not tonight. She already knew what she'd see.

The sixth strip light blinked off just as she neared the underpass exit. She lunged for the orange glow of the streetlights just beyond the tunnel mouth. Before she could reach it, she felt something clamp down hard on her shoulder, spinning her about. She fell backwards out of the tunnel, landing hard on the concrete. At once light and sound exploded around her, the rape alarm screaming at full volume and the torchlight cutting through the gloom like butter. When she switched them both off with shaking hands, she realised an old man was leaning over her. He'd been coming down the ramp just as she burst from the underpass, and she'd almost knocked his walking stick out from under him.

"Are you alright, miss?" he asked.

"Someone was chasing me!" she gasped, pointing with trembling fingers into the underpass. "He..."

She trailed off when she realised there was absolutely nothing behind her. The sixth light had blinked on again, and with its added illumination, she could see all the way to the other end of the tunnel. It was completely empty. If anything really *had* been there, she would still see it making a dash for the far side. Nothing could move fast enough to have escaped before she looked back. Nothing human, that is.

"I don't see anyone, miss. Was he in the car park? Is that why you ran down the underpass?"

The old man's frown looked a little too much like the way her mother silently concern-trolled her over the dinner table for her to want to confide in him further.

"No, I… Never mind. I think it was just my imagination. Thanks anyway for stopping."

Helen pulled herself up and shoved her rape alarm and torch in her bag so she wouldn't look completely paranoid as she walked to her building. She hurried away without offering to walk the old man through the underpass. She'd seen him in the newsagent shop on the other side of the estate before, so she knew he was a local. And if he looked at her like she'd lost her mind when she said she was being followed, then he'd clearly never seen the shadow himself, or anything else of concern in the underpass.

That must mean it was just her it was after.

Helen shuddered and tried her best not to run the rest of the way back to her building. She'd had more than enough unwanted exercise for one night. She managed to keep it together as she made her way back through the bleak estate. She managed to stop her hands from shaking by jamming her hands in her pockets in the elevator up to the twelfth floor. She even managed to stop her bottom lip from trembling for long enough to give her next-door neighbour a shaky smile when she passed him in the corridor.

It wasn't until she'd locked her own door behind her and thrown herself down on the couch that she finally let out the wail that had been threatening to choke her. The tears came thick and fast.

First came tears of fear. What was in that awful tunnel? What did it want?

Then came tears of self-pity. Why her? What had she ever done? It wasn't fair.

Next came tears of misery. Why had Kevin treated her like that? She hadn't deserved it.

And finally came tears of regret. Why had she left and moved to this place? Had she overreacted? Would Kevin take her back if she just called him?

Drying her eyes, her hand hovered over the phone. One phone call, that's all her mother said it would take. She knew her mother was right. Kevin was lazy to the core. All those years, it had been *her* pushing him to study, to pass exams, to work. She knew he'd much rather take her back than face the challenge of starting again with a new girlfriend. Meg might be happy to sneak around with him for the excitement of doing something illicit, but she was much too good-looking to settle for someone like Kevin. He was just a gap-filler till she saved up enough to move to the States to pursue her own American dream. She was no long-term threat to Helen's dreams of a white-picket-fence life in their humdrum little home town.

As her hand closed over the phone, Helen felt that strange sensation again, as though the sutures of her broken heart were tugging in two different directions. One half was pulling her home, to the comfort and safety and pretence of a fairytale life. All she had to do was shut her eyes to Kevin's faults and paste on a fake smile and everything would be OK. The other half of her heart was pulling in the opposite direction, to an unknown future she wasn't convinced she wanted. She wasn't sure she could face the uncertainty at the end of the dark tunnel, both the one in real life, and the one in her mind.

Maybe truth was overrated. Maybe she preferred the security of life with Kevin. Their love might be as fake as the wood panelling in their house, and their garden might be filled with more lies than wild roses, but at least it would be safe. Maybe if she just called him…

She summoned up all her willpower, and dropped the phone.

You need to pull yourself together and sort your head out, she told herself sternly.

There was nothing in the tunnel. It was all in her head. She'd always wanted to be a children's author, hadn't she? Hadn't she always made up stories in her head, ever since she was a little girl? Hadn't some of the characters she'd created seemed so real to her she could almost have sworn she'd had conversations with them? This shadow was the same thing. A figment of her overactive imagination, nothing more.

And if it isn't? asked the troublesome little voice at the back of her head.

Well, if it isn't, then I'll deal with it properly, Helen decided. She marched to the kitchen counter and took the smallest, sharpest knife from the block by the cooker.

I'm not putting up with this any longer! she told herself. *If that thing comes at me again, it's going to get what it deserves.*

This time when she fell asleep on the couch with the TV blaring in the background, it was the sharp knife she cradled next to her heart instead of the soft cushion.

The next morning, she slipped the knife into her purse before she left for work. She didn't bother with the torch. It had proved useless against the monster in her mind. The knife would be more effective, in as much as it would at least prove that she was dealing with an illusion rather than something real. After a moment's hesitation, she slipped the rape alarm into her pocket too. It might not work in the tunnel, but it would at least summon help at the other end if she needed it.

There was an edge to her anticipation all through that day at work. She found her fingers drumming repeatedly on the reception desk, her eyes darting around the lobby and her nerves strained to breaking point by the sound of footsteps crossing the corridor to the restaurant. She couldn't focus on the reservations on the computer screen, and she jumped every time the telephone rang. Even her shift supervisor commented on her distraction, which proved how oddly she must be acting, given he'd barely noticed her existence until now.

By the time the hands of the clock had crawled round to eight p.m., Helen was wound so tight she felt like a firework about to go off. She pulled on her winter coat and cradled the purse she hadn't let go of all day. Carrying it and its precious cargo out of the hotel, she crossed the car park, making her way to the steps leading down to the underpass.

The night was sharper than ever, the frost nipping her fingers as she stood under the dim streetlamp, staring down at the tunnel below. She felt the same sick feeling in the pit of her stomach that had troubled her as a child, when she'd had a recurring nightmare every night for three months. Her mother had told her she simply had to put up with it, just like she urged Helen to put up with Kevin's philandering. Her father had told her she'd grow out of it, just like he insisted Kevin would grow out of chasing other women. She'd learned a valuable lesson at that young age: there would be no help from those closest to her. She was on her own with the monsters in the dark, and if she wanted them to go away, she'd have to deal with them herself.

She pulled the knife from her purse, crossing the bag's strap over her head and body to make sure it wouldn't get in the way if she needed to use the blade. She pulled the rape alarm from her pocket and held it in one hand. Clutching the handle of the kitchen knife tightly in the other, she descended the stairs and headed into the tunnel.

The first strip light was buzzing loudly, while the one at the far end was flickering in warning. Helen gritted her teeth. She knew what she had to do. If she didn't deal with her fears now, they'd forever plague her. Whatever this illusion was – whether a trick of the light in the tunnel or a product of the mental stress she'd been under – she had to prove once and for all that the shadow wasn't real.

Her heels clicked loudly down the concrete tunnel. Her sensible shoes hadn't proved any more effective in helping her run to safety, and tonight she daren't risk carrying a change of footwear in a bag that might make wielding a knife more tricky.

She regretted that decision the moment she felt the

hair on the back of her neck start to prickle.

Not yet not yet not yet, she told herself, forcing herself to stare straight ahead as she broke into a run. She knew it was behind her. She knew it was closing in. She could feel the atmosphere of the tunnel become charged with malevolent intent as the thing tried to reach her before she escaped. She was so focussed on the tunnel exit, she only realised she'd automatically pressed the rape alarm switch when she heard the 'woo, woo, woo' wailing over the pounding of blood in her ears. The yawning tunnel walls distorted the sound as it bounced between them, becoming a high-pitched voice that shrieked, "You... You... You..." all around her as she ran.

Her fear reached such a fever pitch, she'd almost forgotten she was carrying a knife when the force clamped down on her shoulder just as she reached the other end of the tunnel.

This time, she managed to keep her balance as she was spun around.

Her hand shot out automatically to push at the thing behind her.

The hand with the knife.

The pulsing shadow looming over her felt strangely solid as the knife plunged deep into its core. The dark shape seemed to vibrate frantically, as though in some kind of other-worldly death throws. Although it was more like an absence of light than an actual form, she had the strange impression of eyes gazing back at her, widened in fear, just like her own. Just as the shadow melted away like smoke, the rape alarm died in her hand, its last wailing 'woo' so soft it sounded like a single word being gasped in shock.

"*You..!*"

The sixth light above her flickered back to life. Helen blinked. The tunnel behind her was empty, the unsettling atmosphere evaporating just as the shadow had. She knew now with absolute certainty there was nothing to be afraid of anymore. It was gone for good, and it seemed to have taken all of her problems, doubts and fears with it. Shoving her silent rape alarm and knife back in her purse, she felt unaccountably light as she stepped out of the underpass and walked up the ramp to the road.

The uncomfortable feeling that her heart had been split in two was gone. The sutures had healed and she was whole again. Everything seemed so clear now.

She knew what she had to do.

This time her haste to get back to her apartment came from eagerness rather than fear. As soon as she was through her front door, she reached for the phone and dialled the number she knew as well as she knew her own name.

"Hello?" a gruff voice at the other end said. Her new

number was obviously not familiar. That didn't matter. She wouldn't need to use it for much longer. Just hearing a single word from the voice that sounded like safety and comfort and home was enough to convince her beyond any doubt that she was making the right choice.

"Hello, Kevin? It's Helen. Look, I know things have been difficult between us these last few weeks, but I just wanted to say that I'm over that now. I've made some silly choices and done some things I regret, but I hope you can forgive me for running away like that. I'm done running. I want to come home."

There was silence at the other end for a long moment, then Kevin spoke again, his voice sounding strained like he was holding in a strong emotion that threatened to overpower it. "You mean that, Helen? You'd be willing to give it another shot?"

"Yes. We can talk about it in person."

"When?" There was excitement in Kevin's voice now, something she hadn't heard from him in many years.

"I have to work one final shift tomorrow – the other receptionist timetabled for this week left early today as she's sick, so I don't think she'll be in tomorrow. It wouldn't be fair to walk away without covering that one shift, especially as I don't plan on working my agreed notice period. I'll get the bus first thing on

Wednesday morning. Can you pick me up when I get home?"

Home. That word was music to Helen's ears.

"Do you want me to take you to your parents' house?" Kevin asked. The question had a hidden subtext that Helen instantly understood.

"No. I want to go *home.* With you. Is that OK?"

Images of the snug, wood-panelled house flooded Helen's head. The wild roses would be shrivelled and dead by now, but it might not be too late to plant some winter bulbs. She could finish painting the nursery, and she and Kevin could have a small wedding reception in the New Year instead of the lavish Christmas affair they'd originally planned. It would all work out, her dream life. She couldn't believe now that she'd nearly thrown it all away.

"That would be wonderful, Helen," Kevin said. "Just let me know when your bus gets in and I'll meet you at the station."

"I'm looking forward to it," Helen said, unable to stop herself from smiling. "I missed you."

"I missed you too, love. See you soon."

When Helen put the phone down, she wasn't filled with loneliness and regret the way she'd been every night for the last few weeks. She felt at peace with herself. She felt at one with her future, ready to embrace it and Kevin, flaws and all.

She didn't waste time in front of the TV. She packed up the few belongings she'd brought, wheeling the two suitcases to the door, ready for departure. Just one more day, one last shift, and then she'd be going home to the place she belonged. It seemed so simple now she couldn't believe she'd ever had doubts before.

That night she slept so peacefully she was almost late for work. She barely thought about her previous experiences as she raced through the underpass to get to the hotel just in time to take over from the sleepy night-shift manager. Her cheery greeting seemed to surprise him. He clearly wasn't used to hearing enthusiasm in her voice.

Helen's good mood lasted all day. She smiled at every hotel guest no matter how rude or unreasonable they were, she made an extra-special effort to speak to the cleaners at breaktime despite their limited English, and she even went out of her way to help the obnoxious day-shift manager sort out a booking problem with a local taxi company. She didn't mention she was leaving the next morning, though. She'd phoned the other receptionist who'd assured her she'd be back in tomorrow, so she knew the desk would be covered in her absence, and she didn't want to explain her reason for leaving to the day-shift manager in person.

At the end of her shift, Helen collected her coat and

purse from the staffroom, waited until the day-shift manager had gone upstairs to deal with a guest who had a problem with their room, then tiptoed into the office to place her resignation letter on the manager's desk. She didn't look back as she crossed the lobby and hurried into the car park. She didn't want to say goodbye to anyone. She'd prefer not to take part in a pantomime where staff members who barely knew her name acted as though they were sorry she was quitting.

It wasn't until she got to the top of the steps at the far end of the car park that she realised she still had the knife in her bag. She'd been so busy packing last night it hadn't even occurred to her. She unzipped her purse and stared at the small blade inside that glinted in the streetlight's orange glow. She wasn't afraid she'd see the shadow tonight. There was nothing in that underpass that could hurt her now.

But still...

She passed her purse strap over her head like she had the previous night and kept it unzipped. Caution had become habit, and it was better to be safe than sorry on this final trip through the tunnel that had troubled her every waking moment since the end of her first hotel shift.

Confident there would be nothing to see tonight, Helen walked down the steps, her head held high.

As soon as she entered the underpass, she saw it.

This time the shadow wasn't behind her, it was ahead of her. Pulsing into view in the middle of the tunnel, the dark vibrating shape made by an absence of light was moving not towards her, but away from her.

It seemed to be heading for the far end of the underpass, to the circle of orange light at the tunnel mouth. But tonight there was no disturbing atmosphere in the underpass, no sinister feeling of malevolent intent trapped between the curving tunnel walls.

Maybe, Helen thought, *it's because the shadow is just a woman like me.*

It was an odd thought, and she wasn't sure where it came from. But the more she stared at the figure ahead of her, the more convinced she became that it was the pulsing outline of a woman that was moving through the tunnel.

Another realisation followed close on the heels of the first: Helen was angry at that shadow woman. She was so, *so* angry at the weeks of misery and fear she'd had to endure. It was all that shadow woman's fault. That thing, whatever it was, owed her. Helen wasn't quite sure what it owed – an apology? Some kind of compensation? She didn't know. All she was sure of, was that she couldn't let this shadow woman reach the end of the tunnel and melt into the night without confronting her.

Taking the knife from her purse as a precaution, Helen

broke into a run down the underpass. There was an odd moment as, up ahead, the shadow seemed to pause. The dark entity changed shape, its top half vibrating in Helen's direction, almost as if the figure was looking round at her. Then the shadow's passage down the tunnel suddenly increased in momentum, as though the figure had worked out Helen intended to catch it.

You're not escaping, not after everything you've put me through! Helen thought, her cheeks so hot with anger she felt like a star going supernova as she ran down the tunnel. Her whole being was focussed on catching that shadowy figure and making it pay for what she'd endured these last few weeks. She couldn't let it escape.

She caught it just as it reached the mouth of the tunnel.

Helen's hand reached out, grabbing for the pulsing shape. For a moment, she was afraid her fingers would simply pass right through the dark figure, but instead, they found purchase, and Helen pulled, tugging the shadow back into the tunnel before it made it across the threshold. The sixth light above them was dead. Silhouetted by the glowing orange circle outside, the dark shape seemed to spin around. Helen was ready. Her knife was raised. It was her turn to…

Oh.

It felt at first like a punch to the chest. The shadow

had pulsed faster as it turned, lashing out. Helen looked down.

There was a knife sticking out of her chest, cutting right through her heart.

Darkness closed in, black spots swimming at the edge of her vision and converging until all she saw was a narrow circle of light at the tunnel mouth. Framed by that orange glow, the figure was thrown into sharp relief for just a single moment.

And at last, Helen understood. She finally worked out what the shadow was, and why it was following her.

Staring into the terrified eyes of the woman – the woman she herself had been just the night before – she knew why everything had seemed so simple then, and exactly how the complex duality of her real life and dream life had come to be resolved.

Just as her heart stopped beating and the world faded from view, Helen breathed her last, her final word a mocking echo of the sound she'd heard when she'd naively believed she'd defeated her shadow.

"*You!*" she gasped.

TUNNEL VISION

The Garden of Friedan

Terry and Janet Dixon both agreed that their neighbour's garden had got out of hand.

It wasn't really old Finnigan Friedan's fault. There wasn't much he could do about it now that he was dead. But, as Janet repeatedly complained to her sister on their weekly phone calls, the old man really should have made an effort to sort his affairs out while he was still alive. Ever since he'd suffered a fatal heart attack three years ago, his estranged son and daughter had been fighting over the property in court. Not that Terry and Janet had ever seen either of the junior Friedans in person. They hadn't even bothered to make an appearance at their father's poorly attended cremation. That had been left to Mr and Mrs Dixon to organise. Janet made a big show of reading poignant poems at the short service and handing out expensive vol-au-vents at the finger buffet held in the Dixons' conservatory afterwards, but some of the looser-tongued residents of Silver Birch Heights whispered it was less to ease her pain at the old man's passing than to assuage her guilt at failing to notice Finnigan Friedan's corpse mouldering on the kitchen floor next door for three whole weeks before the postman finally called the police.

When the gossiping guests had finally left, the Dixons were left with a mountain of wild mushroom galettes and smoked aubergine canapés, a four o'clock wine headache, and the thorny problem of what to do with the jar of ashes that was sitting on their living room mantlepiece.

"Can't we just post it to one of his children?" Terry had asked, eying the stainless-steel container with distaste. "The least they could do is take charge of their father's remains."

"I've tried contacting them," Janet sighed. "But his son didn't reply, and his daughter sent a letter through her lawyer washing her hands of any funeral expenses. They don't want their father's remains any more than we do."

"Well, it can't just sit there on the mantelpiece forever," Terry frowned.

That was another of the many things the Dixons agreed on.

The next day, Terry and Janet scattered the ashes in their former neighbour's front garden.

"He'll be happy here, amongst the azaleas," Janet said, doing her best to summon up a fake tear to water the old man's remains.

Terry glanced at the withered plants dubiously, but

decided not to spoil the solemn mood by pointing out that half the plants in the garden were clearly dead too.

Finnigan Friedan had been a sprightly, green-fingered pensioner who'd loved nothing more than pottering for hours in the flower beds at the front of his house. Like the other residents of Silver Birch Heights, who hid their decidedly lower-middle-class incomes behind their pretentious property names and mock-Georgian facades, old Mr Friedan had kept up the pretence of affluence through a carefully maintained garden. It didn't matter that the gardens of Silver Birch Heights consisted of little more than postage-stamp lawns fringed by narrow flower beds in front of poorly glazed bay windows which let in the winter wind. What mattered, was how well they were maintained.

Well-kept gardens signalled wealth to this lower-middle-class community. A regularly mowed lawn, weed-free flowerbeds and carefully pruned cherry blossoms told everyone that a property owner either had the leisure time to spend in their garden, or could afford to employ someone to do the work for them. Either way, it spoke favourably of disposable time and income. An untidy garden was not to be tolerated in Silver Birch Heights. It pulled the tone of the whole neighbourhood down.

And when a newly arrived couple moved in to the last house but one and loudly telegraphed their lack of leisure time and disposable income by concreting over the postage-stamp lawn and replacing the flower beds with large ceramic planters, the whole community had signalled their disapproval by shunning the offending couple and refusing to acknowledge their existence with so much as a greetings card at Christmas.

Finnigan Friedan had been rightly proud of his garden. He trimmed the lush grass every week, cut back the cherry blossom to ensure the branches arching over his path didn't encroach on the Dixons' property, and pruned the rhododendron bushes so regularly on his half of the flowerbed separating the Friedan residence from number nine next door, that Terry and Janet never had cause to insist on a dividing fence.

It was an oversight they had come to regret over the past twelve years.

They'd never been on familiar-enough terms with Mr Friedan to exchange more than pleasantries on passing and the obligatory cards at Christmas. They'd been quite deliberate about that. Terry worked in an insurance office and Janet was very proud of her part-time job as a receptionist at the local doctor's surgery. Finnigan Friedan, on the other hand, had spent his life fixing up and selling used cars. Not that there was anything wrong with manual labour or working in sales, *per se*, Janet was very quick to remind the Braithwaites who played bridge with her and Terry every

Thursday evening. It's just that one liked to associate with the same class of people, and there was something ever so slightly *grubby* about manual labour and sales. It was a relief to find that after retirement twelve years ago, Mr Friedan confined his grubbiness to his green fingers instead of filling his back yard with spare parts. Janet had been worried that with all that extra time on his hands, he'd take to tinkering with engines, and the yard next to the Dixons' newly built conservatory would be turned into a scrap merchant's playground.

Mercifully, Finnigan Friedan turned all his attention to living things. Starved of human attention, with his wife long dead and his children grown too important to notice their ageing father, he poured all of his unrequited affections into his plants. For the first four years, his garden was picture perfect, the jewel in the Silver Birch Heights crown. Over the next few years, however, Terry and Janet began to notice a number of worrying signs that all was not well with old Mr Friedan – neither his health, nor his finances. It started with the weekly grass-trimmings pared back to once a fortnight, then dwindling to once a month. Over the next few years, the flowerbeds became overgrown, the border plants sprawling over the edge of the public footpath and the cherry blossom branches over-shooting the lawn and beginning to encroach on the Dixons' imaginary line between the houses. Things finally came to a head when the unpruned rhododendron bushes flowered profusely on both sides of the dividing flowerbed. The purple blooms might be pretty, but they were also parasites that were sucking the life out of the Dixons' carefully tended foxtrot lilies.

At his wife's urging, Terry took the unprecedented step of knocking on Finnigan Friedan's front door to discuss the untenable situation with the old man. There had been the sound of slow shuffling from within, and the key had taken what seemed like an age to turn in the inner lock. When old Mr Friedan had finally opened the door, it was clear he wasn't well. His face was jaundiced and haggard, and his hands had stiffened into arthritic claws. Terry had done his best to convey his objections to the state of the garden under the guise of concern for the old man's health, but it was clear from the way Mr Friedan wheezed that he'd be gardening no more, and that medical bills would eat up any chance of employing someone to undertake the work for him.

Returning to relay the sorry state of affairs to Janet, he dispelled her gloom over the deteriorating garden reflecting badly on their own property with the sunny hope that Mr Friedan wouldn't have long to live, that his estranged children, having homes of their own, would speedily sell the property to new owners, and that they, whoever they turned out to be, would make taming the garden their top priority.

Terry Dixon was wrong on both counts.

Finnigan Friedan lived another five years. And after Terry and Janet had scattered his ashes in his front garden, they waited anther three years while his estranged son and daughter squabbled over the property he'd not only neglected physically, but legally in his failure to make a will. At last, with no end in sight, and with the encroaching wilderness now impeding passage to their own front door, Terry and Janet decided the time had come to take matters into their own hands.

"They can't object to us cutting back the rhododendron bushes," Janet said as she and Terry stood one Sunday in their matching gardening outfits, surveying the full extent of the wilderness that more closely resembled primeval forest than lower-middle-class suburbia. "If we can just pare everything back to the dividing line, then people will know the neglect has nothing to do with us."

Janet knew all the members of the community had been whispering about the blight on their otherwise pristine suburban landscape, and blaming the Dixons for not doing more to tame the overgrown eyesore adjoining their property. And if there was one thing Janet Dixon hated, it was being the subject of gossip. She'd endured more of it than she could stomach – the snide comments over lunch with the other ladies of Silver Birch Heights, the whispered disapproval when neighbours passed their house, the sideways glances thrown their way at the Crichtons' annual Christmas party. When the Braithwaites announced last week that they'd no longer be coming over for bridge due to 'other commitments', Janet had finally had enough.

Standing on her own neat lawn with her secateurs in one hand and the electric shears in the other, she felt a rush of excitement at the thought of finally taking control of the situation.

"You start on the rhododendrons while I work on my project of sculpting our ornamental hedge," she told Terry, handing him the electric shears. "Clear it all back to the original dividing line. It's time we reclaimed the path to our own front door, not to mention our flowerbed."

"Just to the dividing line?" Terry asked, frowning at the massively overgrown rhododendrons. "What if the legal impasse lasts another few years and the house stays empty all that time?"

Janet's eyes narrowed. Terry had a point. If he was going to spend all that time pruning bushes that weren't even theirs, he might as well make a thorough job of it.

"Pare the bushes back as far as you can to keep them from our side of the flowerbed for the foreseeable future,"

Janet advised, giving her husband free reign with the electric shears. "The Friedans aren't likely to ever inspect the house before they put it on the market anyway, and the new owners won't know what was here before. Best to cut everything down to size to ensure whoever moves in next will keep everything neat."

Emboldened by his wife's encouragement, Terry set to work with his electric shears, reclaiming first the path from the gate to their front door, then their flowerbed which contained the smothered remains of once glorious foxtrot lilies, and finally, an extra few inches for good measure.

When Terry finally stepped back to admire his handiwork, he realised he'd moved the flowerbed boundary more than just the two or three inches he'd been aiming for. The rhododendrons had been cut to the bone, the bushes sheared completely bare on their side of the imaginary dividing line, the deep cuts extending right to the trunks on the far side of the flowerbed. The height of the bushes had been reduced from almost over Terry's head, to barely above his waist. The top and side of the rhododendrons were barely more than twigs extending from the central trunks, with only the overgrown leaves and flowers on the far side giving any hint that they were once mighty bushes.

"Er, you don't think I overdid it a bit?" Terry asked,

wiping the sweat from his brow nervously when his wife finished her delicate pruning job on the other side of their garden and came over to take a look.

"No, I don't," Janet beamed when she saw what he'd done. "I think it's perfect! Well done, darling." She gave him a peck on the cheek and offered to make them both some fresh lemonade as a reward for their hard work.

Reassured, Terry went to fetch the garden-waste bin and began piling as much of the rhododendron cuttings into it as he thought the council pick-up truck would let him get away with.

That evening, they celebrated their small victory over the forces of chaos with a bottle of wine, a bubble bath, and a rare display of unbridled passion in the spare bedroom.

Terry felt rather smug the next day at work as he shuffled paperwork and looked down his nose at all the other office workers whose glum faces silently announced they hadn't enjoyed spicy evenings like the one he'd been treated to.

His good mood, however, evaporated abruptly at lunchtime. His brother called, and the news he delivered was not good.

"What do you mean it's all gone?" Terry gasped, trying to keep his voice down to avoid letting his co-workers know that something was amiss. "How can that have happened? You insisted those stocks were safe as houses!"

"Well, I was wrong, wasn't I?" his brother's nasal voice whined down the phone. "I never have any luck with these things. Six grand gone, just like that! That's half my savings. I don't know what I'm going to tell Kelly. She was dead set on that holiday in Ibiza this summer."

Terry was too shocked at the news to remember to shudder at his younger brother's plebian tastes.

"Is there any hope of recovering it, Ed?" he asked, trying to keep the panic from his voice. "There must be some way to trade the shares, or—"

"There's not," Ed said flatly. "The company's gone bust and the shares aren't worth squat now. Best I can hope for is that my other investments do well over the next year so that Kelly never finds out. That was good advice you gave me about spreading the risk, big brother, thanks," he said more brightly. "I would've put all my eggs in one basket if it wasn't for you. Just as well you weren't daft enough to invest in that useless company when I urged you to, eh? Bet you're glad about that."

"Yes, very glad," Terry said mechanically, feeling sick to his stomach. "Listen, Ed, work's really busy today – I've got to go. Sorry to hear your news, but better luck next time. Say hello to Kelly for me."

Terry just had time to put the phone down and sprint to the bathroom before the chicken sandwich he'd had for lunch came right back up again.

He sat on his knees in the cubicle, staring at the culinary abstract painting he'd adorned the toilet bowl with and wishing for the briefest of moments that he was dead. That, he thought, might be preferable to telling Janet that not only had he listened to his irresponsible brother's hare-brained get-rich-quick scheme, he'd also invested almost every penny of their savings in it. He'd known she'd veto the idea, and Ed had been so persuasive he just couldn't resist the promising opportunity to attain the affluent, securely *middle*-middle-class lifestyle they both aspired to.

"You're a fool," he told his pale reflection in the mirror when he'd finally got himself cleaned up. "And what's more, now you're a poor fool."

He could only hope that his utter dejection would trigger the latent maternal instinct that Janet had never manifested towards their daughter during Katie's early years, and she'd feel sympathy for his boyish regret rather than rage at his childish mistake.

That evening, Janet manifested neither sympathy nor overt anger. But her silent fury was more eloquent than words could have been. It took over two hours of deep-cleaning the kitchen before Janet was calm enough to speak to him again. When she finally came stomping out, she folded her arms and stared contemptuously down at the prone form laid out like an invalid on the sofa.

"What about the mortgage?" she demanded through clenched teeth. "How are we going to pay for the house?"

Terry sat up. If Janet had moved beyond the accusation stage and was now composed enough to discuss the practicalities of their reduced state of affairs while still employing the pronoun 'we', there was hope for their marriage yet.

"We'll need to tighten our belts if we're going to pay all our monthly bills with just our salaries," he told her. "I'll need to work overtime, of course, but I'm sure we can manage with some economising."

He left the distasteful corollary – that Janet would need to work full-time instead of part-time hours from now on – unspoken.

The shared mortification at their new reality hung in the air between them, and Terry could almost smell it poisoning the atmosphere of the once upwardly mobile house as Janet glared back at him.

"I take it our Paris trip this summer is now out of the question?" she snapped.

"I'm afraid so. We could maybe visit your sister in Brighton instead?"

The temperature of the room dropped another ten

degrees.

"What about the spare bedroom? It needs a new carpet."

"That project will need to be put on hold for the time being, I'm afraid."

"We haven't paid off the conservatory yet."

"Ah... I'll need to take out a bank loan to cover that. We should be able to pay off the interest each month if we cancel all our subscriptions and shop more economically." Terry shivered. Janet's stare was glacial, and the room was starting to freeze.

"You mean no decent TV from now on, no going to the gym, no book club, and shopping at the budget store in the industrial park instead of at Willoughby's?"

"Look, I know it'll take some getting used to, but we'll manage if we just—"

"We'll manage financially, perhaps!" Janet cried, her hard exterior finally cracking. "But how on earth am I going to manage the shame of it?"

Terry rubbed a hand across his tired eyes. "Maybe you could ask Katie if Arthur wouldn't mind..." Terry trailed off, realising his mistake when Janet's mouth fell open in shock.

"You are not *seriously* suggesting we tell our daughter that you've blown any chance of a decent inheritance from us, and go begging cap in hand to our son-in-law, are you?" Janet gasped.

Terry shook his head vigorously. He and Janet had both come from working-class roots. Their modest house with its middle-class pretensions had been a source of great satisfaction to them, but their real pride and joy was their daughter, Katie. She hadn't just done well in life, she'd exceeded their highest expectations. Not quite academic enough for a degree in medicine, but with solid grades and a far more caring side than her mother, Katie had gone to nursing school and then on to a job at the regional hospital. There, she'd caught the eye of a talented resident surgeon, whom she'd married five years ago.

Terry secretly wondered if it wasn't their boasting about their golden daughter and her beautiful home in the exclusive Poplar Meadows estate that had put their hitherto friendly neighbours' noses out of joint rather than the sprawling mess of the garden next door. He didn't voice his concerns to Janet, though. He was too proud of Katie himself to stop bragging about her wonderful life and handsome surgeon husband. He had noticed of late, however, that his stories about the dinner parties he attended in Poplar Meadows and the doctors and lawyers he'd hobnobbed with there had been met by barbed condolences on his conspicuous lack of grandchildren.

It was a source of even greater concern for Katie. Five years married and still no sign of the longed-for children she'd been dreaming of since she was a little girl. Terry knew that Janet had quietly suggested a check-up with the doctor and the possibility of IVF, but Katie had shut down any mention of the subject. Terry had a suspicion that despite his years of training in the field, Arthur's pride was too fragile to subject his manhood to medical scrutiny in case the problem lay with him. Whatever the reason for their lack of reproductive success, Katie was growing so sad it almost broke his heart to see. If she didn't have a child of her own soon, Terry worried that—

"Terry, are you listening to me?" Janet demanded, dragging his attention back to the problem at hand. "I asked when you're going to the bank to see about that loan?"

"Tomorrow lunchtime," Terry said quickly. "I'll go to the branch opposite the office."

And that's exactly what he did. It took several nerve-racking weeks for the application to be approved given their reduced circumstances, but when the money had finally passed through their account and on to the building company to settle the conservatory debt, Terry breathed a long sigh of relief.

The respite from his worries didn't last long. The bill was paid on a Wednesday, and by the following Friday, Janet was back to pacing around the house all evening like a polar bear trapped in a zoo.

"Just look at that!" she tutted, twitching the bedroom curtains aside and pointing into their front garden. "Look at those branches!"

Terry had hoped the hack-job on the rhododendron bushes would be enough to take her mind off the fact that the cherry blossom tree had overshot its own garden by so much it was now blocking the light to their upstairs rooms. He didn't want to admit he didn't have the wherewithal to deal with this problem either.

"Come back to bed, my love," he coaxed. "We're only up here at night when the curtains are closed, so what difference does it make?"

As usual, he'd said the wrong thing.

"What difference does it make if old Friedan's jungle has got so out of control we can't even see out our own bloody windows? Are you serious?" Janet snapped.

Terry winced. Janet only ever swore when her rage overcame her penchant for middle-class affectation.

"I can't sort it out for the moment, my love. Those branches are so thick I'd need a chainsaw to get through them, and the only person I know who has one is Simon Braithwaite."

"Then borrow his," Janet told her husband. "He'll be so happy you're finally getting off your arse and sorting that bloody garden, he might even deign to join us for bridge again."

"Don't be coarse, my love," Terry sighed as Janet slouched off to the bathroom and he sunk back under the sheets to contemplate his new problem. He couldn't ask Simon Braithwaite for his diesel-powered chainsaw. If he did, Simon would ask about the money Terry owed him. Unbeknown to their wives, Terry and Simon had been betting on their bridge games for years. Before the breakup of the regular Thursday-night meetings, Terry had racked up a very tidy sum in gambling debts. He'd told himself he was simply on a losing streak and his luck would change. But before it did, Lydia Braithwaite had taken umbrage at the deteriorating state of their neighbour's garden, and had laid the blame for the decline in standards in Silver Birch Heights squarely at the feet of the Dixons.

It had almost been a relief to Terry to see the back of Simon Braithwaite for a while. He'd thought it would give him time to shuffle money between accounts so that Janet wouldn't notice the shortfall. That was when they'd *had* money. Now that it was all gone, Terry had an even more pressing reason to avoid Simon.

The thought of how he was going to manage the gambling debt on top of all his other bills, *and* manage Janet's dissatisfaction at the state of old Friedan's garden, kept him awake for half the night.

When he returned from the office the next day, exhausted from working the Saturday overtime shift and desperate for dinner after skipping lunch to save money, the first thing that Janet said when he walked through the door was, "Well? Didn't you notice?"

"Notice what?" he asked, peering over her shoulder and hoping she meant she'd somehow rustled up a roast on their shoe-string budget rather than the unappetising casserole of miscellaneous half-price vegetables he was swiftly learning to loathe.

Janet rolled her eyes at him. "The *garden*, of course."

Terry felt a flash of panic. Janet hadn't gone round to the Braithwaites' and borrowed the chainsaw herself, had she? And if she had, Simon wouldn't have casually hinted that it was about time Terry honoured his debts, would he?

Before he could ask any incriminating questions that would arouse Janet's suspicions, his wife took him by the arm and led him back outside to stand on their front doorstep.

"There." Janet pointed next door. "Isn't that much better?"

Terry glanced nervously at the sprawling cherry blossom tree. Its branches were intact, the withered flowers generously sprinkled around their own garden in dusty heaps now that the promising April had given way to an unpleasantly hot May. He breathed a sigh of relief. Janet hadn't gone to the Braithwaites' house after all.

"Um, yes, that's wonderful, Janet, well done," he nodded at her.

"You have no idea what I've just spent the last five hours on, have you?" There was a dangerous edge to her voice.

"Of course I do!" Terry glanced back over the truncated rhododendron bushes, hoping to spot the blindingly obvious before Janet lost her temper. Then he noticed the grass, and his nervous smiled widened into a genuine grin. "The lawn looks so much better now."

His praise was genuine too. The grass, which until now had more closely resembled a field of sickly wheat than the lawn of a housing estate with genteel pretentions, had finally been tamed. Going by her blistered fingers and sunburnt nose, Janet must have spent all Saturday afternoon chopping the prairie-like stems down to a manageable size before raking the cuttings out of the way and running their mower over the remains. The formerly lush lawn was now little more than a patchwork of yellow stubble in soil long-since sucked dry of all nutrients, but it looked a damn sight better than it had the day before.

"You're an angel," Terry beamed at her, giving her a tentative peck on the cheek.

"And don't you forget it," she growled back.

Janet's self-satisfaction lasted all of twenty-four hours.

That's when she first began to notice that her hair was falling out.

It was the shriek from the bathroom that Sunday night which alerted Terry to the problem. He jumped out of bed and ran down the hall to find Janet leaning over the sink, staring wide-eyed into the mirror with a clump of dyed-blonde hair clutched in her shaking hand. "What's happening to me?" she gasped. "My hair's falling out!"

"Don't worry about that, my love," Terry soothed, putting his arms around her. "Mine fell out years ago. I know it's an unpleasant reminder that we're both getting on a bit, but—"

"Terry, I swear to God I will shove this hair in your big mouth and make you eat it if you don't shut up right now!" Janet snapped.

Terry almost swallowed his tongue in his haste to comply with his wife's wishes.

"This is your fault!" Janet wailed, pointing at the hairbrush on the shelf that was so clogged with yellow and grey strands that it looked more like a Yorkshire terrier.

"Yes, my love," Terry murmured, figuring this was the safest response.

"It's the stress of losing all our savings and living like paupers, that's what's causing this!"

Terry patted her head gingerly so as not to dislodge

any more loose strands and hurried back to bed without conceding that particular point.

Over the next few days, Janet's shoulder-length mane fell out clump by clump until she was left with a pink scalp and a few last strands of hair that clung incongruously to her head like errant TV aerials. Terry choked down any jokes he might have been tempted to make about the possibility she could make up for cancelling their multi-channel subscription by picking up their neighbours' signals. He knew that would go down like the Titanic, given his wife's shattered self-esteem.

"It's not as bad as all that, my love," he soothed, holding Janet tightly as she sobbed on his shoulder. "If it's going to make you self-conscious, then we can get you some nice wigs. Weren't you always saying you wished you had the nerve to experiment with your hair the way that Grace Malone down the street does? Well, this is your chance! You could wear a curly one, or try that fashionable little... What did you call it? A bob cut? You could give that a go and see if it suited. That way, once your hair grows back in, you'll know exactly how to style it."

"You think so?" Janet sniffed.

Terry wasn't sure if she was asking if he thought she could find a style that suited her or if he thought there was a chance her hair would actually grow back in, but he nodded anyway.

Janet took a week off work while she waited for her mail-order wigs to arrive, both unfortunate expenses they could ill afford, but Terry took it on the chin and worked even more overtime hours to compensate. Seeing a brave smile back on his wife's face when she tried on her new bobbed wig was worth the tension headache he'd come home with every day that week.

"You don't think it looks fake, do you?" she asked, turning this way and that to see it from all angles in the bedroom mirror.

"I think it looks wonderful on you," Terry said, with as much enthusiasm as he could muster in his exhausted state.

"Really?"

"Really," he repeated.

"Really?"

Terry realised that Janet had turned away from the dressing table mirror and was throwing him a coy look from under her new fringe.

Oh, dear God, not tonight, Terry thought to himself. His back ached, his head was thumping, and if he lay down for more than half a second he felt sure he'd pass right out. On the other hand, if he didn't perform for his wife, she'd doubtless take it as direct evidence that she'd lost all attraction in his eyes along with her hair, and he could kiss his marriage goodbye. He'd just about survived driving a wrecking ball through their family finances. Turning his wife's advances down when her ego was so fragile, however, would be martial suicide.

Trying not to grimace as his back screamed in protest, he let Janet climb aboard and have her way with him until she'd satisfied herself that her middle-aged attractions were not diminished by her sudden and unseasonable moulting. When she was finally done and snoring loudly, her wig on its stand and her bald head on her pillow, Terry limped to the bathroom in search of the strongest painkillers he could find. Gulping down five at once, he made a mental note to ask his boss tomorrow if he could have one of the new ergonomic desk chairs the managers had bought for their department meetings.

He didn't get the chair. What he *did* get, was a dressing down from his line manager for handing in shoddy work over the past few weeks, and a stern warning from the suits upstairs about rumours that he'd been seen nodding off with his head on the desk in the afternoons.

Mercifully, the next day was Sunday, and although he was desperate for the chance to catch up on sleep, he wouldn't pass up his daughter's invitation to lunch for the world, even if it did mean getting up early to wash and wax the car so as not to attract the scorn of the Poplar Meadows' residents.

Janet was understandably nervous on the drive over, repeatedly pulling a mirror from her handbag and checking her wig. Terry said, "You look lovely, Janet," so many times he was afraid he'd developed a verbal tic and that he'd blurt it out the next time his line manager called for his opinion at a team meeting. But it reassured Janet to hear that her synthetic bob looked chic, and that her decidedly upper-middle-class son-in-law wouldn't look down his nose at it.

As it turned out, Arthur barely deigned to raise his nose from his newspaper at their arrival, and so looking down it was out of the question. His behaviour towards his parents-in-law had cooled significantly since the early days of wooing and wedding his wife, and Terry sincerely hoped it didn't signal a change in his affections for their daughter. Certainly, his bland indifference to Katie's suggestion they eat lunch in their spacious garden's gazebo didn't seem particularly out of character, considering how little Arthur cared for the combination of sandwiches and small talk. But Terry kept a wary eye on his son-in-law during lunch all the same, alert for any signs of unusual coldness towards Katie. Given how little attention he generally paid her, and how often he had his nose buried in a paper or a book, it was difficult to tell if today's behaviour betrayed any hints of future martial failure.

Janet, as usual, made up for her son-in-law's silence.

Once she'd received enough compliments from her daughter on her new 'hair cut' and thrice repeated the fictional account of the hours it took her stylist to get it just right, she moved on to the more weighty matters of the dreadful behaviour of patients at the doctor's surgery these days, the latest gossip from Silver Birch Heights, and the ongoing concern that the late Finnigan Friedan's garden was causing.

Having noted with relief that his daughter didn't intend to question her mother's account of how she came by her clearly synthetic wig, Terry had nodded off under the gazebo, only to be rudely awakened by the mention of old Friedan's garden.

"Not *this* again, Janet," he said gently but firmly, patting his wife's hand and hoping she'd take the hint. "I'm sure Katie and Arthur are tired of hearing about it." That wasn't entirely true, as Arthur hadn't paid the slightest bit of attention to their tales of garden woes in the three years since old Friedan died, but he thought it was only proper to include his son-in-law all the same.

"But it's such a worry!" Janet said petulantly. "Honestly, Katie, you should see how long the branches of that awful cherry blossom have grown – they're right across our upstairs windows! They block the light so badly it's like mid-winter upstairs, even in the height of summer."

"Can't you just cut them down?" Katie suggested

reasonably. "If there's no designated owner to get permission from, then I don't see why you can't remove obstructions on your own property. What do you think, Arthur?"

"Whatever you say, dear," Arthur sighed without looking up from his paper.

"The garden next door's mostly under control after the work we've done there over the last month," Terry said quickly, hoping to change the subject. "But enough about that, we want to hear about the holiday you're planning to—"

"Those branches have got to go, Terry," Janet interrupted. "I don't know why you won't ask Simon Braithwaite to lend you his chainsaw. I asked you a whole week ago. Grace Malone's husband spends an hour in their garden every evening. He never needs to be asked twice to get anything done."

Grace Malone's husband, Terry thought irritably, *spends an hour in the garden every evening and all weekend in the pub because he can't stand his horse-faced nag of a wife.*

Terry's eyes darted around his daughter's beautifully laid-out garden, searching for something new to praise to avoid discussing the cherry blossom tree. He couldn't reveal the real reason for his refusal to talk to Simon Braithwaite. That would lead to the subject of his gambling debt. His inability to pay it would lead to the subject of his recent financial losses. Janet had made it clear he was not to mention that particular embarrassment to Katie and Arthur under any circumstances.

"Are you OK, Dad?" Katie asked, frowning as her father wriggled uncomfortably in his delicately carved garden chair. "You look like you've got a sore back."

Terry grimaced. That was another subject he daren't touch on. His sore back would lead to the subject of the overtime he was working in his rickety office chair, which would lead straight back to the subject of his recent financial losses. His eyes took on a slightly panicked look as they cast about for something else to comment on.

"You should let Arthur take a look at that," Katie said, her brow furrowing at the pained expression on her father's face. "He's an absolute whiz when it comes to back problems. Arthur, could you—"

"Would you like to borrow my chainsaw, Terry?" Arthur said suddenly, looking up from his paper to head off his wife's unwelcome request.

"That would be wonderful, thank you!" Janet replied for both of them. "That's very generous, Arthur. It'll be such a weight off my mind when we finally get that problem sorted. Thank him, Terry," she urged with a sideways frown at her husband.

"Thank you, Arthur," Terry repeated dutifully, resenting his wife's insinuation that he was a five year old without manners.

"I don't think you should be using a chainsaw with your back in its current condition, Dad," Katie worried. "Maybe Arthur could pop round next time he gets a day off, and he could—"

"It's very easy to use, and the exercise would be good for stretching any tight muscles." Arthur cut her off before she could commit him to an insufferable afternoon at his in-laws' house which he'd only visited twice in the whole time they'd been married. "Besides, work's very busy at the moment, what with the upcoming promotion and everything."

"Of course!" Katie clapped her hands in delight. "I completely forgot to tell you our news!"

You haven't manged to get a word in edgeways for the last hour and a half, that's why, Terry thought, throwing his wife a sour glance when she wasn't looking.

"Arthur's going to be made chief of surgery when Doctor Miller retires at the end of the month! Isn't that wonderful?" Katie beamed.

"That's amazing!" Janet cried, almost knocking over her teacup in excitement. Terry's own joy at his daughter's good fortune was genuine, but if he was being completely honest, he was particularly buoyed up by the hope that his son-in-law's pay rise might encourage him to look more favourably on the request for a loan Terry had determined to make.

Not today, though, Terry thought to himself. *Not while Katie and Janet are here.*

The borrowed chainsaw would give him the perfect opportunity to catch Arthur alone when he drove back to return it.

If Terry thought bringing the chainsaw home would be enough to put Janet's mind at rest for a while, he was dead wrong. As soon as they got back to Silver Birch Heights and Terry hoisted the heavy saw from the car along with the can of petrol he'd borrowed, Janet asked, "Aren't you going to sort the tree this afternoon?"

"I wasn't planning on it – it is nearly four o'clock after all," Terry said. "I was going to put it in the shed for now. I'll maybe have time next weekend."

"But there's hours of daylight left, and after all those sandwiches at Katie's, we can have a late dinner," his wife protested.

"Janet, my back's killing me," Terry sighed. "I've been doing overtime for weeks now in that bloody awful desk chair that digs into my spine all day long. I've had a non-stop tension headache for the last fortnight, and don't even get me started on the pain in my—"

"Well, whose fault is that?" Janet snapped. "If you hadn't gone and... Well, hello, Mrs Cartwright. How are the grandchildren?" She veered off topic, her scowl changing to a fake smile as an elderly lady came plodding through the quiet cul-de-sac pushing her walker frame ahead of her and allowing her pint-sized dog to pee on the wheels of the parked cars.

"Yes, it is hot today, isn't it?" the deaf old lady smiled back.

Despite the impossibility of her hearing anything the Dixons were saying, Janet waited until Mrs Cartwright had crossed the street and disappeared down one of the little lanes crisscrossing Silver Birch Heights before continuing her rant in lowered tones.

"Look, if you can't be bothered doing it, just say so. I can do it myself – I seem to be left to do everything these days, so one more job won't make a difference. Give it here." Janet held her hands out for the chainsaw.

Terry winced, but the pain came from more than just his back. While he resented the implication that he wasn't pulling his weight, seeing the determined look in his wife's eyes and the way she was bravely battling to keep up appearances despite the wig that was sitting at a decidedly wonky angle in the afternoon heat, his heart ached for everything she'd lost.

"It's not a problem, my love," he said gently. "I'll get it done before dinner."

"Thanks Terry. I do love you, you know."

"I know you do."

Hurrying upstairs to change into his gardening clothes,

Terry resolved to sort out the problem of old Friedan's overgrown vegetation once and for all. It wasn't enough to just trim the cherry blossom branches back to the notional line dividing their adjoining properties. If the court case wasn't decided within the next year or two, they'd be right back to square one. And even if the house went on the market soon, the new owners might fall in love with the way the cherry blossom ached over their path, and insist on keeping the branches right on the boundary between the houses. Terry could foresee future trouble if those branches ever crossed one inch into the Dixons' space. After all the years of anxiety Janet had suffered, she wouldn't tolerate the slightest infraction on their property again, and there would be war in Silver Birch Heights.

No, better to cut the tree right back to where it belongs – on the lawn in front of the window, Terry thought. He could still remember the first time he'd seen that tree, when the Dixons had moved in decades ago. It was just a short sapling then, its thin trunk held upright by a post sunk into the circle of soil in the centre of the lawn. It had been planted by Finnigan Friedan's wife, just like the rhododendrons and most of the perennials. That was why old Friedan had tended them so lovingly after he retired.

Well, I'm sorry, old man, Terry thought, setting up his ladder on the lawn next door, *but I'm just cutting it back to its original proportions. Nothing more.*

The job took him far longer than he thought it would. Dinner time came and went, and it was almost dark by the time he'd lopped the final branch. He was glad the light was fading as he switched off the chainsaw and folded up the ladder. He didn't want to see clearly the devastation he'd wrought on the once magnificent tree. He'd originally intended to cut the branches back to the edge of the lawn, but climbing up and down the steps and moving the ladder around was too much for his back. He'd settled for positioning it at the bottom of the tree and cutting the branches off at the point they forked from the trunk.

He worried now he'd overdone it. The tree would take years to produce flowers from the spindly twigs that would grow from the pollarded stumps. It would never regain its former glory. And given how deeply Terry's chainsaw had bitten into its core, it might never recover at all.

Terry looked away from the amputated branches that lay scattered across the lawn. He felt slightly sick at what he'd done. His back was too sore now to clear up the mess, so he had to make do with just moving the longest branches that were flattening the rhododendron bushes. If he left those ones for even a day, their combined weight might kill off the bushes he'd hacked down too. He tried not to listen to the voice that told him he should have contented himself with just trimming those overhanging branches and let the rest of the tree be. It was too late now.

Janet's smile when he returned sweaty and aching went some way to soothing the misgivings he was having. Following his progress from their bedroom window, she had nothing but praise for the decisive action he'd taken to forestall any issues they might have with their next-door neighbours in the future.

"The garden's almost presentable now, even if it is dry as a bone," Janet smiled happily at him over their late dinner of overcooked vegetable hotpot.

"Almost?" Terry felt his heart sinking at that single foreboding word.

"The azaleas will need to be pulled up – they're all hideously withered. And the plants bordering the public footpath will all need to go too – they're so overgrown they're getting in the way of prams and wheelchairs. In fact, it would be best if the flowerbeds were all stripped and weeded so the new owners can start fresh when the house finally gets sold, don't you think?"

Seeing her husband's face turn pale at the thought of the mammoth task ahead, she said quickly, "But don't worry, I know your back's playing up. Once we've arranged for the council truck to pick up the tree branches, I can manage the rest."

"But you're working full time now too, my love," Terry

protested.

"That still leaves me an hour or two more free time than you have," Janet told him. "We're so close to taming that wilderness, it would be a shame to stop now. I'm going to finish it, even it takes me all month."

Terry smiled proudly at his wife across the dinner table. Once she set her mind to something, there was nothing Janet couldn't accomplish.

They didn't get to enjoy their victory over the forces of chaos for long, however. All Monday morning at work, Terry had the nagging feeling that something was terribly wrong. By lunchtime, his nebulous fears had grown such long arms and legs, it felt like his mind was being colonised by some otherworldy creature composed entirely of dread.

As soon as the clock on the wall above his line manager's desk hit noon, Terry snatched up the phone and dialled his wife's work number. Janet – juggling a queue of grumbling patients, a stack of mislabelled prescriptions, and a junior staff member who kept mixing up the medical records – was not best pleased to hear that her husband had called her for no reason.

"What do you mean 'nothing's wrong but you're calling to check'?" she demanded. "I have my hands full here. We don't get a full hour's paid lunch-time like you, you know."

"Sorry, Janet, I just… Sorry."

Terry put the phone down. After a moment's hesitation, he called Katie at the hospital where she and Arthur both worked. It took ten minutes for his call to be re-routed to the right department, then another fifteen before Katie could be found.

"Dad, what's the matter?" she asked when the charge nurse finally located her and directed her to the phone in the nurses' station. "Has something happened?"

"No, no, don't worry," Terry said quickly. "I'm just calling to see if everything's alright?"

"Of course it is, why wouldn't it be?" The concern in his daughter's voice made him feel far worse than his wife's irritation had.

"No reason. Sorry, pet. I'll see you soon, OK?"

"OK, Dad. Take care."

Terry could hear that she wanted to press him further to find the reason for his strange behaviour, but she was too busy, and now was not the time.

Despite reassurances from both his wife and daughter, Terry still felt the foot soldiers of unnamed dread continuing their march up his spine to make camp in the fear centre of his brain. He wasn't sure he'd win an all-out war with the primitive forces of terror in his head. He had to find the root cause before he completely lost his mind.

With ten minutes of lunch-hour left, he tried phoning his brother, Ed.

His wife, Kelly, answered the call. “Lazy bastard’s upstairs asleep,” she complained. “Lost another job, hasn’t he? Only held on to this one for three weeks before he got the boot. Can you believe it, after all he put me through with that get-rich-quick scam he fell for, losing all our money, and now he can’t even hold on to paid work for a single month together without—”

Terry extricated himself from that unpleasant conversation as quickly as he could without actually putting the phone down on her.

Five minutes left. Only one person he hadn’t checked.

He couldn’t stand Janet’s sister, Ruby, and if Janet was being honest, neither could she. But if anything happened to Ruby, Terry knew that Janet would be inconsolable, and the thought of her grief was more than he could bear. For Janet’s sake, he dug deep, and phoned Ruby.

“Hi, I’m not in at the moment, but if you leave a message after the tone, I’ll get back to you as soon as I can.”

Terry put the phone down before the answering-machine tone sounded. He’d forgotten Ruby was spending a week on a bus tour of Italy. Ruby was several years older than Janet, and had taken early retirement. She took too many holidays on her small pension, and always ended the year with a request for funds from her sister. That would have to stop, given the Dixons' own financial constraints. But in the meantime...

Terry bit his lip. Had something happened to Ruby? Was that why he was feeling this terrible dread? Maybe he should ask Janet to call her hotel to check if—

"Daydreaming again, Dixon?"

Terry's line manager stopped beside his desk and glared down at him. "You know our department's next in line for a round of compulsory redundancies, don't you? The powers-that-be will make their final decision about who's for the chop next week."

He left the threat hanging in the air and marched off to terrorise one of the secretaries into photocopying faster and fetching him coffee.

For the chop...

That phrase echoed ominously in Terry's head, accompanied by the drone of a chainsaw and the crash of falling branches.

Maybe that's all it is, he thought. *I'm still feeling guilty about that damn tree and it's stressing me out. I have to stop beating myself up about it. It needed cut, and that's all there is to it.*

Terry hunched over his desk for the rest of the afternoon, trying to concentrate on writing reports instead of worrying about things that couldn't be helped. By the time he'd made it to half seven, his back was spasming from sitting for so long, and his stomach was cramping with hunger. He'd been so busy phoning people he hadn't had time for lunch, and the overtime hours meant it was long past his usual dinner time.

The drive home felt like it took a million years instead of forty-five minutes.

As he turned up the hill to Silver Birch Heights and passed the houses facing the main road, he couldn't help glancing at number eight next door to his own home. The sight of the garden littered with dead cherry-blossom boughs was bad enough, but it was the tree trunk with its crown of stumps where once magnificent branches had been that really made him shudder.

It needed to be done, Terry repeated to himself, turning in to the cul-de-sac behind the row of houses. *I didn't do anything wrong.*

The feeling of dread finally crystallised, however, when he walked into his living room to find Janet slumped on the sofa sobbing her heart out.

"Janet! What on earth's the matter?" he cried. "Is it Ruby? Have you heard news from Italy? Is she—"

"Ruby?" Janet gazed at him with red-rimmed eyes. "No! It's Arthur! There's been such a terrible accident at the hospital!"

Janet's words were drowned out by another wave of

sobbing, and it wasn't until Terry had fetched her a cup of sweet tea and hugged her for a good fifteen minutes that he was finally able to get the news out of her.

"There was a fault with the elevator he was travelling to the operating theatre in," Janet hiccupped. "It got stuck part-way down, between floors four and five. When the doors opened, there was only enough room to crawl through. Arthur should have waited until the maintenance team came to fix it, but the operation he'd been called to was an emergency, and he was only thinking of the patient waiting on the table. So he... he..."

Janet took another gulp of tea, and Terry fought the urge to shake the rest of the story out of her.

"Stay calm, my love," he urged, though his own hands were trembling. "What happened next?"

"Well, he'd just put his arms out to crawl through the gap to get onto the fifth floor, when... I don't know how, but…"

"Janet, what happened?" Terry could feel his heart about to explode in his chest with the tension.

"The elevator suddenly dropped down to the floor below. And with Arthur's arms halfway out the door, they were…"

Janet didn't need to say the rest. The sickened look on her face was enough.

Terry put his head in his hands. There would be no

chief of surgery position now. The best Katie could hope for was that Arthur had been prudent enough to take out medical insurance, and that the compensation payments from the hospital would tide them over until such a time as Arthur recovered enough physically to take up work as a G.P. in a local practice. That is, if he recovered from his ordeal mentally. And he would need support from now on for everyday tasks, and Katie would have to…

Terry groaned aloud, his daughter's golden future dimming in his mind's eye to one of difficulty and despair.

"I should never have done it!" he whispered. "I should never have cut that damn tree! I knew as soon as I had that we'd be made to pay somehow."

He hadn't realised he'd spoken aloud until Janet asked, "What's that, Terry? What about the tree?"

"Nothing, my love. We should drive to the hospital to be with Katie. She needs us right now."

Katie needed her parents for more than just that one long night at the hospital. It was many weeks before Arthur could come home, and that was just the first step on a long road that would lead to physical therapy, prosthetics fittings, and intensive psychological counselling.

The next month passed in a blur. Janet switched back to part-time work to support their daughter, and

Terry, having already maxed out his overtime hours at the insurance office, took on an evening job in a call centre. His days now started with rising at five a.m., getting to the office for half six, working until seven-thirty, then walking down the high street to the call centre sandwiched between the multi-story car park and the travellers' hotel. There, he worked from 8 p.m. until midnight, reaching home to collapse into bed at one in the morning for a few hours of broken sleep before beginning it all again the next day.

By the end of the month, he was starting to think he was hallucinating with exhaustion. Every time he passed by in the car, the garden of Number Eight Silver Birch Heights seemed to be more overgrown than ever. The Braithwaites had kindly paid for the tree branches to be uplifted by a gardening firm, but Terry suspected that was less out of compassion for their family's plight and more out of irritation at the debris littering their otherwise tidy estate. While the remains of the tree were stark and bare, and the rhododendron bushes were clearly dead on the Dixons' side where they had been hacked back to the bone, the rest of the garden seemed to be growing more like a jungle every day.

Which was odd, because there'd been so little rain that June, the plants were looking withered and parched despite getting bigger and bigger.

Lost in the fog of his own overworked mind, Terry

had come to dread the sight of old Friedan's garden, dark thoughts swirling through his head every time he caught a glimpse of the pollarded tree stumps and rhododendron bushes that had been hacked down and spliced in half.

Each time the Dixons had meddled with the garden next door, there had been consequences.

Don't be so foolish! The reasonable part of Terry's mind told him. *Those were simply coincidences. Plants can't make things happen in the real world. We've been unlucky, that's all.*

But then again...

He'd lost his savings the day after he reduced the rhododendron bushes to a pale shadow of their former glory. His wife had lost her hair the day after she'd hacked the grass and shaved the lawn down to stubble. And the day after he'd lopped the cherry tree branches off, Arthur had lost…

Stop it! It's coincidence! Nothing more!

When Janet phoned him at work one Friday morning, seven weeks after the accident, Terry feared the worst.

"What is it, Janet? Is it Katie? Is it Arthur? Has something happened to them?"

"It's the most wonderful news, Terry!"

The joy and excitement in his wife's voice almost melted Terry into a sticky puddle of relief on his office chair.

"You'll never guess what! Katie's pregnant at last! Isn't that amazing?"

Terry *was* thrilled at the news, both for Katie, and for himself and Janet, but he couldn't help wondering how Arthur was going to cope with a new baby now that he...

No. He mustn't think like that. This was the first good thing that had happened for a long time, and he wasn't going to spoil it with any doom and gloom.

"I just had to call and tell you straight away. Katie didn't say a word about it until she asked me to go with her for the twelve-week scan today. Everything's looking just fine on the sonogram – I can show you the picture when you get back tonight. You've got the evening off the call centre, haven't you?"

"Yes, they're redecorating the building and switching out the equipment, so all the call handlers on our floor have to make up the time next week."

While Terry was overjoyed at the thought of the night off, he was not looking forward to the Sunday shift he'd have to cover the following week.

"Perfect, then I'll pick up a bottle of bubbly for us to celebrate tonight. And I'll make something extra-special for dinner. You deserve a change from roast vegetables and hotpot."

Terry thanked her and put the phone down, trying not to resent the fact that his wife was only working three days a week now. She had been round at Katie's house every day, helping her deal with the emotional fallout of Arthur's accident, after all. Terry didn't envy her that particular chore. On balance, he'd rather be breaking his back in the insurance office and call centre six-and-a-half days a week.

Seeing his line manager frowning in his direction, and having only narrowly survived the most recent round of redundancies due to working so much overtime, Terry put his head down and returned to his financial reports.

His mind couldn't help wandering during the long day, though.

A baby in the family would be wonderful, and just what Katie needed to focus her mind on right now.

And he was looking forward to that bottle of bubbly and special meal Janet was preparing for him. In fact, he was looking forward to it so much, he had to keep reminding himself to stick to the speed limits on the drive home. The Dixons were so far under water financially, that one speeding ticket could sink the whole family boat.

Janet was so elated when he arrived home, at first he thought she must have started on the champagne without him.

"Don't be silly, of course I wouldn't open it before you got back," she laughed at him. "And I'll show you the wonderful sonogram picture in just a moment, but first, you *must* see what I've been spending the whole day on since I got back from Katie's check-up."

"Weren't you at Katie's house today?" Terry asked. "I thought you were planning to help her clear out that spare room on the top floor?"

"We'll do that tomorrow instead," Janet told him. "She went with Arthur to couple's counselling today so they could discuss the issues he's having adjusting to things. With their new baby on the way and everything, I thought I should give them some space to talk things through privately rather than hovering the background all afternoon."

Terry blinked at his wife, wondering if news of the baby at the clinic had also come with a free personality transplant for his wife. Passing up the chance to hover in the background and get on everyone's nerves was so out of character he had to open the fridge to double check the cork was still in the champagne bottle and this wasn't just the drink talking.

"So what did you spend the afternoon doing instead?" he asked, noticing his wife getting impatient with his lack of curiosity

"Not just this afternoon. The rest of the morning, the afternoon, and most of the evening too. I've only just come in and changed. Come and see!

And just like that, the bubble of happiness Terry had

been floating in burst. He knew now, with dreadful certainty, what Janet had been doing. He'd been so focused on getting home to the champagne and the special meal, that for once, he'd driven past Number Eight Silver Birch Heights without glancing over at the garden.

Now, standing on their front doorstep and looking over the dying rhododendron hedge, Terry could see everything clearly. The late July air was hot and stuffy, the evening sunbeams dancing on the dust that still hadn't settled after the day's upheaval. Every flowerbed had been stripped, the dry soil turned over and the withered plants piled in enormous heaps on the stubbly lawn. Their long roots protruded like dead cables detached from the nerve centre of a digital plant, the garden now devoid of any life to support.

"What do you think?" Janet waved at the scene of devastation, proud of her handiwork and eager for praise.

Terry could only nod dumbly, his eyes glazed in shock.

"Hmph, well, I know you're tired, so maybe that champagne will wake you up a bit," his wife frowned, putting his lack of rapture at her efforts down to overwork on Terry's part.

The special dinner Janet had prepared of roast beef and Yorkshire pudding sat heavily in Terry's roiling stomach, and a second glass of champagne was enough to bring it all back up again just as he was brushing his teeth before bed. He ran both taps to cover the noise of his heaving, hoping Janet wouldn't hear him. He didn't want to worry her, not after everything she'd been through.

How can I stop something terrible happening in the next twenty-four hours? he asked himself, wiping his lips with toilet paper and gargling with mouthwash to get rid of the taste of bile on his tongue. *There must be something I can do!*

He didn't ask himself what terrible things might happen next as a result of Janet's attack on old Friedan's garden and the plants his late wife had lovingly tended all those years ago. He already knew.

An image of a tiny life forming in the grainy sonogram photo flashed through his mind, and he dry-heaved again at the thought of what would inevitably follow if he didn't find a way to stop it.

There must be something I can do! he told himself again as he lay awake all night, listening to Janet snoring peacefully for the first time in months. *There must be something!*

By the time the morning sun was peeking through the bedroom curtains, Terry had made up his mind. Dressing quickly and kissing his sleeping wife on the top of her bald head, he hurried out to the car and drove to work.

He only stayed until ten, making sure to tell everyone loudly and repeatedly how ill he was feeling. By mid-morning, his line manager had heard enough, and told Terry to take a sick day and go home.

Terry left the office double-quick time, but he didn't return home. Not straight away. First, he went to the small shop on the far side of town that had an array of crystal balls and strange-looking herbs arranged on velvet drapes in the window. He'd noticed it when he and Janet had come out of the theatre across the road one evening, several years ago now. He remembered it, because he'd pointed it out to Janet and laughed at how credulous some people were.

He wasn't laughing now.

He tried peering through the window to get a sense of what was inside, but he couldn't see anything past the heavy drapes. Only the 'open' sign hanging on the door told him the business – whatever it might be – was still up and running.

Terry wasn't sure what the protocol for such places was. Should he knock and wait for the door to be answered from the inside? Should he go in and announce himself? Or should—

"Oh, sorry, love." A young woman with pink hair and a nose ring flung open the door and stepped out, almost tripping over Terry as he stood hesitating on the pavement. "Come for a love potion too, have you?" she cackled, holding up a brown paper bag full of something foul-smelling. "You should try Stacey's passion-fruit blend – does the trick every time!"

She waved the bag at him and walked off, leaving Terry feeling decidedly let-down that his last hope was now in the hands of a woman called Stacey who sold smelly love spells to students from the local art school.

Still, with no other options and very little time, Terry knew he had to give this outside hope a try. Pushing the door open again, he stepped gingerly inside the shop. He wasn't sure what he'd been expecting – something that looked more... mystical perhaps. There had been an effort made to create something approaching an enchanted atmosphere with the judicious placement of coloured lamps around the shop floor, whose glow made up for the lack of light from the curtained window and door. However, the effect was somewhat spoiled by the tacky displays of plastic dreamcatchers, artificial crystals, cheap mood rings and scented candles cluttering the shelves.

"Can I help you with anything, my dear?"

Terry looked over at the woman standing behind the counter. She was dressed in a velvet skirt and peasant blouse that were two sizes too big for her skinny frame, and she was at least three decades too young to be addressing him as 'my dear'. Terry's heart sank.

"Are you Stacey?" he asked.

"I am, my dear. Are you here for something in particular? A palm reading? Tarot? Perhaps a love spell? Or if it's a present you're looking for, we do a lovely range of scented candles and crystal paper-weights."

Terry decided against asking if she was an art student too. It wouldn't help to know just how underqualified this shop assistant was. He needed something to believe in right now, and if believing Stacey was a trained psychic with a direct link to the other world would help him win the fight against old Friedan's garden, then he would be her most devoted disciple.

"Do you have anything for…" Terry paused, not quite sure how to frame his request.

"Problem downstairs, is it?" Stacey threw a pointed look at his belt before glancing lower.

"No! Nothing like that. Not downstairs, but next door."

Stacey's look turned blank.

"What I mean is, I'm having problems with my neighbour's garden," Terry hurried on, his explanation sounding garbled even to his own ears. "It's the plants, you see – they've become overgrown, and my wife and I have been trying to—"

"Garden centre's down the block," Stacey interrupted,

a bored look on her face as she turned to flick through a catalogue on the counter. “Weedkiller’s half price this week, so my boyfriend tells me. He works there.”

Terry tried again. “No, no, it’s *destroying* the plants that’s been *causing* the problems. Ever since the previous owner died, the plants seem to be… I’m not sure how to put it. Taking revenge on anyone who interferes with them?”

Stacey closed her catalogue with a thump, gazing back at Terry with an eager glint in her eyes now. “Ah! I see. Well, in that case, I think I have exactly what you need. Come to the back of the shop – that’s where we keep all the special herbs.”

Half an hour later, his wallet considerably lighter, Terry was driving home with a brown paper bag full of dried plants on the passenger seat next to him.

He fixed his eyes on the road as he passed the row of houses leading to his own cul-de-sac. He wasn’t sure why, but he had the sneaky suspicion that the garden of number eight could read his intentions from a distance.

You’re becoming paranoid, he told himself as he parked the car by his own back gate.

Are you, though? the other voice – the one that had disturbed him for months now – whispered back. *You know what happens when you mess with that garden. You can’t take any chances, for Katie’ sake.*

It was the thought of his daughter and her baby that

gave Terry the courage to rummage around in the kitchen drawer until he found a box of matches and a handful of firelighter cubes left over from a previous barbecue.

"Terry, is that you home?" Janet's voice called down the stairs as he walked to the front door.

"Janet? What are you doing here? I thought you were helping Katie with her spare room?"

"I am." Janet appeared at the top of the stairs, gazing down at him in concern. "I just popped back to collect one of our old photo albums. Katie wants to make a collage for the new nursery, and she thought it would be cute to include some pictures of herself when she was a baby. What are you doing back home, Terry?"

"Um…"

Terry's mind raced. If he invented an illness, Janet would follow him around for the rest of the day like a mother hen, trying to force-feed him vegetable soup and nagging him to rest. But if he told her the real reason, he was scared she'd either think he was mad, or worse, believe him and go mad herself with panic.

His eyes came to rest on the new camera that was still sitting in its box on the hall table. An idea finally flashed through his tired head. It was a stroke of inspiration.

"Friedan Junior's solicitor called me at work today,"

he said casually, opening the camera box. "He asked if I could take some pictures of number eight for the court files he's preparing – just of the outside, of course. It would save him making the trip from London if I could send them over, and he needs them right away."

"Oh." With little experience of such matters, Janet was willing to take her husband's word for it. "But what about work? Don't they mind you taking the time off? If you'd just called me, I could have taken the pictures."

"I've done a lot of overtime recently, so my line manager didn't mind me asking for a few unpaid hours to take care of things," Terry said breezily. "Besides, the solicitor's job comes with a fee, and that'll make up for the unpaid hours. *More* than make up for them," he added, when Janet still didn't look convinced.

"I see. Well, I suppose it's nice we'll get to eat lunch together before I go back to Poplar Meadows and you go back to work." Janet's face brightened. "We haven't had lunch together since... oh, I can't remember when! You go and take the pictures, and I'll make us some nice sandwiches – we still have some roast beef left, so I'll make meat slices, how does that sound?"

"Perfect, my love," Terry said, hoping that this time, he'd be able to keep the roast beef down.

Closing the front door behind him, he crossed the path and stepped over the dying rhododendron bushes into the garden of number eight. Checking to make sure

Janet wasn't looking out of the window, he set the camera down carefully on the stubbly lawn next to one of the uprooted piles of dry plants. The new camera had been ordered for their holiday in Paris that summer. He'd remembered to cancel the holiday booking, but forgot all about the camera until it arrived last week. He'd been intending to return it for a refund, but Janet had pleaded with him to keep it so they'd have high definition photos of the baby when it came. Terry had thought they needed the money too badly, and not reaching an agreement, they'd left the camera sitting in the hall while they argued over its fate.

He was glad now he'd forgotten to take it back to the shop this morning like he'd been intending to. It was the very excuse he'd needed to get this job done without arousing Janet's suspicions. He just hoped none of the other neighbours would notice his strange behaviour in the garden of number eight before he managed to finish it.

Pulling the bag of dried herbs from his coat where he'd hidden it, he arranged them in a circle on the stubbly lawn according to the diagram Stacey had sketched for him, and placed a firelighter cube at each compass point along the rim. He set the small cubes alight one by one with his matches, then, taking a deep breath, he began to recite the verses Stacey had printed off for him.

Terry had never studied Latin, so not only was he unsure what he was saying, he was also unsure if he was saying whatever it was correctly. His confidence hadn't been boosted by the fact that Stacey seemed to have got the spell from a dog-eared library book titled 'Spells-4-U', but the herbs smelt potent, and right now he was desperate enough to try anything.

He'd just finished reciting the final line, when there was a hissing sound from the grass, as though a hundred snakes were slithering through the stubble. Terry glanced down. From where he stood in the centre of the circle of burning herbs, he could see the lawn undulating below his feet. It began gently at first, but then the piles of dry plants that Janet had torn up began to topple in all directions as the ground beneath them roiled, the dusty soil of the flowerbeds churning as though an unseen hoe was digging up the dirt. The crippled cherry tree began to shake violently, a loud creaking coming from inside the trunk.

It's working! Terry thought to himself, feeling the air crackle with electricity around him. *Whatever those herbs are doing, the spell is working!*

He was just about to give a loud whoop of relief, and damn what the neighbours might think, when Janet came racing from the front door of their house.

"Terry!" she shrieked, her face pale with fear. "Terry! Come quickly! It's Katie!"

Terry dropped the box of matches in horror and leapt back over the dying rhododendron bushes.

The next four hours passed in a blur.

There was a panic-stricken drive to the hospital.

A long wait until a doctor finally came to talk to them.

Twenty minutes of sobbing and another ten trying to dry up any evidence of tears.

A visit to Katie's room with brave faces pasted on.

An hour sitting with her and Arthur until the doctor came back to tell them Katie needed to rest.

And then a dismal drive home, this time with no hopes of a baby next year to signal the start of spring.

I don't understand it, Terry thought to himself as he gripped the steering wheel with clenched fists and stared at the road ahead. *I know I was sceptical about Stacey's spell, but it did seem to be working. What on earth went wrong? Was it the herbs? Was it my reading? Was it—*

"Oh, God, Terry – look!" Janet cried, her hand flying to her mouth as they drove up the hill to Silver Birch Heights.

Black smoke wreathed the street on which numbers eight and nine stood.

For one awful moment, Terry felt sure his house had burned to the ground.

Then they reached the crest of hill, and they saw more

clearly that the fire had been limited to the garden of number eight. The bay windows were scorched and the front of the house was blackened, but the blaze thankfully hadn't touched their house next door before the assembled fire fighters had managed to douse the flames.

Their car tore round the cul-de-sac, and Terry and Janet ran to find out what had transpired in their absence.

"Seems the fire started in the garden next door," one of the firefighters told them as he wound the long hose back up. "You're lucky one of the neighbours called when they did – those plants were so dry they went up like a pile of kindling in the summer sun. Another ten minutes, and the blaze would've crossed over to your property. There's little we could've done if the fire had spread from the garden to the houses. Do you have the contact details for the owner? Someone said the house is being contested in court?"

The crowd of neighbours who were gathered in the cul-de-sac to watch the goings-on all started talking at once, relaying the story of the old man and his estranged offspring, and the court case that was dragging on, until one of the firefighters help up his hand and said, "Sorry, we've got another call. Got to go."

"And you're sure it was just the summer heat that set

the garden on fire? Terry asked loudly. He couldn't believe now he'd left a circle of herbs burning in a garden full of dry plants, and his conscience prickled painfully when he remembered the box of matches he'd dropped. "It's a common occurrence at this time of year, is it?"

"Yes, though we won't be able to confirm that until the investigator gets here. She's on her way now – she should arrive within the hour."

Terry nodded, hoping that would give him enough time to locate any trace of the fire lighters, herbs and matchbox, and eliminate himself as an arson suspect. He'd been so focused on the spell, it hadn't even occurred to him that the herbs might start a fire. If he'd thought he could get rid of the whole garden that easily, he would have just—

A strange wind stirred the street, catching at the clouds of black smoke and sending the assembled neighbours scurrying back to their houses with its sudden chill.

"Come on Terry," Janet sighed, taking him by the arm and leading him to the kitchen where the roast beef sandwiches still sat uneaten on the table. "We both need a nice cup of tea to warm us up."

But it wasn't the heartbreaking events at the hospital or the sudden chill wind that was making Terry shiver. It was the thought that had just occurred to him.

If the spell *had* worked, then Katie wouldn't have lost her baby.

And if the spell *hadn't* worked, now that he'd set the whole garden ablaze, its revenge would be swift and—

"Get the phone, will you, Terry?"

"What?" Terry tore his eyes from the window where he was watching the fire truck drive away, and glanced towards the hall.

The telephone on the table by the coat rack was ringing loudly.

"The phone." Janet pointed with the knife she was cutting the sandwiches with. "I've got butter on my hands."

The phone.

The phone that rang to give news of Arthur's accident.

The phone that rang to tell them their daughter had lost her baby.

The phone that was now ringing right after Terry had set the whole garden of Friedan ablaze.

"Terry! Answer it!"

Terry walked slowly down the hall, his whole world collapsing to the size of the table where the phone lay ringing, ringing, ringing by the front door. The dread filled him so completely he felt as though he was drowning in fear. He knew who the call was from. He knew what the caller would say. And he knew, without a shadow of doubt, that the first words he heard on the other end would strip all meaning from his life, just as the life had been stripped from Finnigan Friedan's once beautiful garden.

He picked up the phone with a shaking hand.

"Hello?" he whispered.

The Red, Red Road

Despite the summer heat, Tom felt a chill of fear shiver down his spine when he saw the duty roster for the coming week.

He hadn't been near that road in twenty-five years. Every car journey he'd ever taken since that night, every bus trip, and every single walk with the family dog had been carefully calculated to avoid that stretch of tarmac branching from the main highway to the Burnback Estate. It hadn't been easy. He'd had to move out of his parents' cramped apartment at seventeen, leaving the claustrophobic but familiar council blocks behind and sofa surfing his way down a list of distant acquaintances until he landed a job that paid enough for him to rent a small place of his own. Visiting family and friends left behind had become fraught with difficulty, his routes planned with precision to ensure he took buses that dropped him off on the other side of the estate to avoid the Red Road. When he saved up enough for a car of his own, he parked at the abandoned scrap yard a half hour's walk from his parents' run-down building, despite how risky it was leaving a vehicle unattended for so long in an area filled with disaffected teens, addicts desperate to score their next fix, and dealers looking to make some easy cash on the side.

His parents never questioned his reasons for avoiding the Red Road. No one did. No one from his past, that is. Everyone on the Burnback Estate knew what had happened that night.

At least, they *thought* they did.

They thought they knew what that road represented to Tom, and why he took such pains to avoid it.

But they were all wrong.

Tom knew if they found out what had really happened that night, he wouldn't just lose the trust and respect of the family and friends he'd left behind on the Burnback Estate. He'd also lose the new life he'd made for himself in Kellway Gardens – his wife, his children and his liberty. Prison would be the punishment awaiting him if the truth ever got out – the truth about the terrible deed he'd done when he was young and stupid and hadn't realised that his claustrophobic life on the estate wasn't all the world had to offer, and the future was still ripe with possibility.

As far as everyone was concerned, Tom Jackson was one of those rare Burnback boys who'd made good. He might not have done well in school, and he might have been a bit of a rascal in his early teens, but the tragic events on the Red Road when he was seventeen seemed to have lit a fire under him. He hadn't followed the usual path of the youth from Burnback – relying on government handouts while they drifted from one dysfunctional relationship to another, leaving a trail of unwanted children in their wake as they slid down the ladder from dealers to addicts to dead or jailed by their mid-thirties. No, Tom had moved out, worked his way up to a respectable council job on a road maintenance crew, got married and had two children who, by all accounts, were on track to go to university in a few years.

His parents couldn't have been prouder. And that's why Tom kept his mouth shut when his foreman asked, "Hey Tommy, is there a problem with the rota?"

Tom's eyes slid off the sheet pinned to the notice-board, a fake smile already pasted on his lips as he turned to face his supervisor.

"No problem, Stan. I used to live up that way, so I'll probably get some stick from the Burnback lot for doing council work while they're off to the pub, that's all."

"So you're a local celebrity, then? Worried that the estate girls won't be able to keep their hands off you, are you?" Stan laughed. "I hear those tarts go nuts for a hard hat and a high-vis jacket."

"Yeah? Well, most of them have faces like melted tarmac

and arses to match, so don't get your hopes up for meeting a decent date while we're working next week," Tom shot back.

"Who's talking about dating them?" Stan guffawed, throwing his head back in that wild-dog-howling-at-the-moon way that Tom hated. "As long as they've got their pothole in the right place, that's all my drill needs, eh?"

Tom smiled back wearily. He was sick of the juvenile innuendo and non-stop banter of the road crew, but he knew better than to call Stan or the other men out for it. It was part of the job, and that job earned him a decent-enough wage every month to support a wife who was a cut above the Burnback slappers he'd grown up with, and two kids who actually knew who their father was. He wasn't dumb enough to open his mouth and earn himself a reputation as a sensitive snowflake. That would be a social death sentence on the macho road crew.

But it wasn't Stan's raucous laughter that set his teeth on edge as he shoved his work boots into his locker and pulled on his sports shoes for the drive home. It was the thought of where he'd be working come Monday morning.

The Red Road.

The place he hadn't set foot on since that awful night when—

Tom slammed his locker shut and strode out to the car park. He wasn't going to think about the past. He had everything he could ever want right here in the present. His wife, Claire, was respectable, hard-working and kind, and she was a wonderful mother to their two teenagers. OK, so her rather dull grey eyes didn't have the spark that had flashed in Jasmine's green eyes when she laughed, and over the last twenty years her figure had softened from ripe-melon-full to marshmallow-plump, but she could hardly be expected to compete with the memory of a girl from twenty-five years ago, could she?

Stop thinking about Jasmine, Tom told himself as he stowed his rucksack in his car and got behind the wheel. *It's not good for you to go digging up the past.*

But he couldn't help it. Every time he sat in the driver's seat and gripped the steering wheel, her face flashed through his head. He could still recall every detail: the bright red lips that warned of danger but promised paradise; the tongue that was deliciously soft one moment then sharp as a lash when her temper flared; and the black hair framing beautiful green eyes that widened in shock that night when they realised his car was—

Tom gunned the engine and tore out of the car park, drowning the unwanted memories in a wave of petrol fumes and an undercurrent of burnt rubber.

He managed to forget about that night for a whole hour. Focussing on the mundane tasks of the present, he stopped off at the supermarket for the groceries Claire had asked him to buy, then turned in to the petrol station to fill the car up. On a whim, he grabbed a bunch of carnations from a bucket by the checkout queue. Claire liked little treats now and then. She thought they were romantic. After twenty years of marriage, Tom thought there was nothing less romantic than a bare-minimum gesture of cheap flowers picked up on passing with zero thought put into them, but if it kept Claire happy, then he was willing enough to do the bare minimum.

He put a good deal more thought into his daughter's birthday gift as he drove the rest of the way home. Hannah wanted a proper 'sweet sixteen' party at the pricey hotel in town, complete with a band, a fancy catering crew, and a limousine hire for herself and her best mates. It was going to set him back a small fortune, and he'd already been working the Saturday overtime shift for the last three months to make sure he had enough to cover the two weeks in Spain he'd promised his parents for their anniversary. He was glad now he'd paid for that and they were currently sunning themselves in the Costa del Sol. He didn't want them here during his week working on the Red Road. They'd ask too many questions about how he was feeling, and the last thing he wanted was anyone else knowing how much the thought of that job troubled him.

"Dad!"

Hannah was the first to greet Tom as he parked in the driveway and opened his front door. No matter how many years he'd lived in this pretty house in the town's decidedly middle-class Kellway Gardens, he'd never quite got used to having his own driveaway instead of a shared concrete forecourt, his own front door that didn't open onto a communal hallway smelling of urine, and two whole floors' worth of space instead of his parents' four cramped apartment rooms.

"Dad, did you book the hotel? What about the limo? You know how important the limo is, I won't live it down if my friends' parents have to drive them to the party. Did you—"

"Hannah, pet, I'm just through the door," Tom said wearily, stowing his rucksack neatly in the hall cupboard so his wife wouldn't nag him about his mess. "I'll make sure it's all sorted in time for your birthday, OK?"

"And the limo?" Hannah gave him the little-girl pout that many years of experience had taught him meant he'd get a hug if he said yes, and a tantrum if he said no.

"*And* the limo, though it'll cost me an arm and a leg."

"You're the best, Dad!"

Tom earned the hug he'd wanted from his daughter before she sprinted upstairs to call her friends and tell them the good news. Tom shook his head, but he couldn't help grinning at her teenage enthusiasm as he went to see what Claire was cooking in the kitchen.

As soon as he opened the door, the smell of crisp onions and pan-fried beef made his mouth water. Claire turned and gave him a welcoming smile, her cheeks dimpling when she saw the flowers he was holding. She was no longer pretty, but with two decades of history between them, her comforting presence was like coming home to rest on a favourite plump cushion after a hard day's work. The hug she gave him lacked the energy or the enthusiasm that Hannah's had, but it was soothing none the less.

"Thanks, Tom. Just leave them by the sink and I'll put them in a vase after dinner," she said, pointing with the spatula she was using to turn the beef. "This'll be ready in ten minutes, so it'll be on the table by the time you wash up."

"That sounds lovely, pet. Is Danny back yet?" There was a sudden change in the kitchen's atmosphere, as though a chill wind had blown in despite the balmy evening outside.

"No, he called half an hour ago to say the bus didn't come, so he'll have to wait for the next one. I'll just pop his dinner in the oven and he can have it when he gets in."

Claire's breezy smile didn't slip and her tone didn't change, but Tom could read the disapproval in her eyes, and he knew it was aimed squarely at him, not their son. He nodded without comment and hurried upstairs to get changed. He didn't want to reopen the debate on that subject. Especially not today, when he'd just found out he'd be spending the coming week working on the very road he'd been avoiding for the last twenty-five years of his life.

The atmosphere in the kitchen had warmed again by the time he sat at the table, the renewed energy mostly coming from Hannah who talked excitedly about the plans for her upcoming birthday without pausing to swallow or take a breath. Tom was happy to let her talk without interrupting to remind her how much overtime he'd have to work to cover everything she wanted. He only had one daughter, and she was only going to be sixteen once. Life was short, and he wanted her day to be perfect.

Jasmine didn't make it past sixteen, a voice in his head reminded him. *She was three weeks away from her seventeenth birthday that night. And Chris hadn't long turned seventeen, he—*

Stop it! Tom commanded the voice in his head. *Stop talking about Jasmine and Chris. There's no point now.*

It doesn't matter anymore.

But it *did* matter. It mattered every time Tom got behind the wheel of his car. It mattered every time he took a detour rather than drive down the Red Road to visit his parents on the Burnback Estate, and it mattered every time he looked into old Mrs Henderson's eyes and saw the raw pain the loss of her son still caused after twenty-five long years.

"Tom? Did you hear me?"

Tom looked up to see his wife raising an eyebrow at him across the kitchen table. At some point, Hannah had disappeared back upstairs without him even noticing. He pasted the smile back on his face and said, "Sorry, pet. I was just thinking about Hannah's birthday. What did you say?"

"I asked if you're coming with me to the care home to see my dad tomorrow? It's been a few weeks now, and you know how quickly he forgets who you are when he hasn't seen you for a while."

Tom's heart sank. He might not like wasting his one day off a week visiting an old man who'd made it clear he didn't think Tom was good enough for his daughter, but disappointing Claire was worse.

"Oh... The care home, right. I'm sorry, but I really need to go and see old Mrs Henderson tomorrow. With Mum and Dad away in Spain, there's no one to go and get her shopping for the week."

"Couldn't one of her neighbours go shopping for her?" Claire frowned. "There's hundreds of people living in that horrible Burnback Estate. There must be someone else who could keep an eye on her while your parents are on holiday."

"There's plenty of folk who'd be happy to keep an eye on her," Tom said. "But I wouldn't trust any of them with the money for her shopping. She'd end up living on toast and beans for the next week till my parents got back, and the rest of the cash would go in their own pocket."

Claire shuddered. "What an awful place. I can't believe you had to grow up in that hell hole."

Tom opened his mouth, about to protest that it hadn't been that bad, that his parents had done their best and there were good people on the estate mixed in with the dealers and wasters the council had dumped there. But before he could get the words out, the front door opened, and footsteps stomped down the hall.

Their son Danny stormed into the kitchen, his blond hair stuck to his forehead with sweat and his T-shirt wet with perspiration.

"That's the third time this week the bloody bus has decided it can't be arsed showing up," he snapped, opening the fridge and gulping milk straight from the bottle. "And the one that finally came only went as far as the supermarket on King's Street. I had to walk five bloody miles back in this heat!"

Claire pursed her lips, too upset by her son's discomfort to tell him off for poor manners or bad language. "That's ridiculous," she sighed. "I'll need to phone the bus company on Monday. If they're not going to stick to their timetable, they can't expect—"

"That won't do any good – you think they're going to bother about a few stranded customers in the arse-end of nowhere? The warehouse is too far out of town for them to run a regular service. You think they're going to make a special effort to pick up three or four people on a route no one else uses?"

"There must be more people than that who need a ride," Claire said, hurrying to fetch her son's dinner from the oven. "There's hundreds of people working at that warehouse."

"Yes, but most of them get the shuttlebus that goes the opposite way to the city, and that's no use to me," Danny snapped, throwing himself down at the kitchen table and using one of his mother's fancy napkins to wipe the sweat from his face. "And all the rest of the shift workers at the warehouse have *cars*."

He placed such emphasis on this last word it almost came out as a snarl. Tom continued to chew his beef slowly, doing his best not to rise to the bait. They'd had this fight one too many times now, and he was in danger of losing if he pressed his own weak argument too strongly.

"Couldn't one of them give you a lift?" he asked, trying to sound reasonable. He didn't meet his son's eye. He knew there would be fire blazing there.

"The guys working the weekend and evenings shifts aren't operating a bloody taxi service, Dad!" Danny growled. "None of them live out this way. If you'd just help me buy a second-hand car, I could—"

"We've talked about this, son," Tom said firmly. "The whole point of you working at the warehouse was for you to save up to buy a car yourself."

"No, it wasn't." Danny leaned forward on the table, forcing his father to meet his gaze. "You wouldn't let me learn to drive when I turned seventeen last November because of the cost. I took that job after school and at weekends to pay for my own driving lessons, and we agreed when I passed my test that you'd help me buy a car if I paid for half of it. We *agreed*, Dad. I passed three months ago. THREE. MONTHS. And then you went and changed the goalposts. Told me I had to pay for my own bloody car. I've been stuck working my backside off at that warehouse all through my school exams, and now I'll have to work all summer if I'm ever going to—"

"Look, son, it's been an expensive year, alright?" Tom cut him off before his son's rant could turn into another fight. "Your Grandad's care home bills are sky-high, I promised my own folks they'd get a holiday in Spain this year, and the cost of living has gone up so much that—"

"Don't give me that bollocks!" Danny interrupted with a snort. "I'm not some little kid you can fob off with made-up stories. You're not even paying for Grandad's care-home bills. The council sold his house to pay for his care. Mum told me."

Tom shot his wife a withering look, but she pretended she was too busy pouring gravy over Danny's fried beef to notice.

"And you've worked overtime on Saturdays for months to pay for Nana and Pop's holiday, so that's not coming out of the regular household budget. And Mum's been selling her handmade cards at craft fairs this year, so there's even more money coming in than when you made me the promise in the first place." Danny played his trump card, sitting back and folding his arms to signal his direct challenge to his father.

Tom didn't have any more cards to play. When Danny turned seventeen, he'd tried the 'driving at your age is too dangerous' argument, but since Tom had been driving himself just a few months after he turned seventeen, Danny quite rightly called him a hypocrite. That argument had been wearing particularly thin over the past year as one by one, all of Danny's school friends had learned to drive and bought their first cars.

Then Tom had tried the financial argument – driving lessons were too expensive, and the family just couldn't afford them. Danny had got round that one with his usual determination, finding himself a job at a packing warehouse at the edge of town after school and on weekends. He'd paid for driving lessons himself, parental permission be damned.

Tom had finally resorted to stalling, telling Danny he'd help pay for a car, but his son would have to put up half of the money himself. He'd underestimated just how badly Danny wanted his independence. Danny had doubled his shifts despite studying hard for his end-of-year exams at school, earning the sum that Tom had specified in record time. Now they were locked in a stalemate over the other half Tom had promised to pay, and Tom was out of arguments.

Well, out of arguments he was willing to use, at any rate. There *was* always the truth – the real reason he didn't want his son behind the wheel of a car at seventeen. But that would require telling him about that awful night on the Red Road twenty-five years ago. The version of the story everyone on the Burnback Estate knew was bad enough. But the *real* story, the one only Tom knew, was a secret he was determined to take to his grave.

"We just don't have the cash right now, OK?" Tom said, staring down at his plate and finding his formerly tasty beef had taken on the texture of ashes in his mouth. "You've got a year to go until university, and God knows that's going to be expensive enough."

"But since Danny's paying for half of the cost of a car himself," Claire said, sticking her oar in when it was least wanted, "I don't see why we can't—"

"Danny! There you are!" Hannah came bursting into the kitchen like a whirlwind. "Jenny wants to know if you'll be her date for my party."

Danny rolled his eyes at his sister. "I'm not dating one of your dumb friends. Even if Jenny didn't have a face like the back end of a bus, she's barely legal."

"Don't be mean!" Hannah scowled at him. "She was sixteen months ago. And it's not a *real* date, she just needs someone on her arm for the evening. Darren dumped her last week, and it's going to look really lame if she's the only one coming without a guy. Please? We'll let you ride in the limo with us to the Glenmont Hotel, and I'll even let you pick some of the band's songs if you promise to be nice to her. We're getting Friday's Fling to play – you remember them from that gig at the club last Christmas?"

Danny's mouth fell open. "Dad's paying for you to have a party at the priciest hotel in town, hiring a professional band, and renting a bloody *limo* to drive you all there?"

There was a stony silence that seemed to last an eternity.

Hannah's eyes flicked between her brother and her father, not quite understanding what the problem was. Tom's eyes were still fixed squarely on his plate.

When Claire broke the silence by placing Danny's dinner on the table in front of him, he pushed it away. "I'm not hungry," he growled. "Give it to Hannah. She might as well have two dinners since she's clearly worth double what I'm worth around here."

He pushed past his sister and marched out the front door before his mother could call him back. Hannah, sensing that her parents were about to have a major row, backed out of the kitchen and hurried upstairs again before the storm could break.

*

Tom had been dreading his visit to Mrs Henderson at the Burnback Estate that Sunday. But after enduring a frosty evening with Claire who refused to understand his objections to helping their seventeen-year-old son buy his first car, and the slamming of the front door and angry footsteps on the stairs when Danny returned late from a friend's house, Tom was glad of an excuse to get away from his family for a few hours.

He took his usual circuitous route winding down the backroads to the old scrapyard at the far side of the estate, making sure to park beside one of the thick bushes by the wasteland that partially hid his car from passers-by. He wasn't sure his insurance would cover parking in such an obviously dodgy spot if his car *did* get stolen, but it was either that or drive down the Red Road, and there was no way he was doing *that*.

Well, not until tomorrow, at least.

Tom pushed the unwelcome thought from his head and unloaded the shopping he'd picked up at the supermarket earlier that morning. It was a long trek across the wasteland to the back of the estate, and an absurd route to take while loaded down with shopping bags when there were parking spaces right in front of the tower blocks. But Tom gritted his teeth and trekked over the scrubland, carrying his shopping with his head down, ignoring the occasional dog walker he passed. This wasn't the middle-class suburbia of Kellway Gardens. You didn't smile and say 'Hello' or 'Good Morning' to people you passed on the Burnback Estate. If you did, you were likely to get a suspicious scowl in return if you were lucky, and something considerably harder in the teeth if you weren't.

By the time Tom had walked to the tower block he'd grown up in, taken the stairs to the ninth floor since the elevator wasn't working as usual, and walked to the far end of the corridor where old Mrs Henderson lived, he was sweating as badly as Danny had been the previous night. Although the prickly heat running up his legs did sting his conscience on his son's behalf, it didn't shake his determination to stall his son's car ownership for as long as humanly possible.

His determination only became more fixed by the footsteps shuffling to the door and the cry of "Chris! You're back!" from the old lady who opened it.

"It's not Chris, Mrs Henderson," Tom said gently. "It's Tom Jackson. I've come with your shopping."

"Oh..." The old lady squinted at him through eyes hazy with cataracts, her joy evaporating when her daydreams faded and the present swam back into focus. "Hello, Tom. It was good of you to come," she sighed. "You were always such a nice boy. That's why my Chris liked you so much. Come in and have a cup of tea."

Tom followed her into the cramped apartment filled with too many cats and a jumble of litter boxes that hadn't been cleaned since his parents went on holiday. He knew his mother came down once a week to help straighten Mrs Henderson's place out, even though her own back gave her trouble these days and her hands were clawed with arthritis. It wasn't just kindness on his mother's part. It was also guilt. They'd both had sons the same age, but Sandra Jackson's son had grown up, found a steady job, got married and had a family, while Maggie Henderson's son would stay forever seventeen in his mother's fading memory.

It was unfair.

And if anyone ever found out just *how* unfair that night on the Red Road had been, Tom would have far more to fear from the Burnback Estate than the thought of his car getting stolen.

He helped Mrs Henderson make tea in her tiny kitchen, rinsing out stained mugs and replacing the rancid milk in her fridge with fresh bottles. He put the rest of the shopping away while the kettle boiled, making sure everything was placed on the lowest shelves where she could reach the packets and cans, before carrying the mugs of tea into the claustrophobic living room. Every surface was cluttered with chipped ornaments, tangles of half-finished knitting, newspapers, or cushions clawed to tatters by the army of cats that slunk their way through the rooms, their eyes narrowed at him in suspicion.

"How has your health been, Mrs Henderson?" Tom asked as he sat down on one of the rickety old chairs. "Have you been keeping well?"

"Oh, I'm fine. Your mother makes sure I take my pills and reminds me when my doctor's appointments are. She's always been so kind," Mrs Henderson smiled at him. "And how's your Jasmine doing? Is she still as pretty as ever?"

Tom's mug stopped halfway to his mouth, his spine tingling as though a bolt of electricity had shot through him. Before he could correct the old lady, she went on, "Jasmine was always such a beautiful girl. My Chris was jealous that you were with her, you know. You and Chris were such good friends, and she nearly came between you. But after what happened that night, I'm glad it was you who married her, and not someone else. Chris wouldn't have liked that. He would have wanted you to be happy."

Mrs Henderson stared into her steaming mug, her spectacles misting and her mind fogging over.

Tom hated correcting her. But he couldn't bear to hear Jasmine's name. An image of her that night flashed though his mind. Two figures standing by the side of the road, their their faces illuminated in the headlamps, their guilty looks turning to horror when they realised the car was bearing down on them.

Tom's hand shook and he placed his mug down on the coffee table with a thump.

"I didn't marry Jasmine, Mrs Henderson," he said, struggling to keep his voice from shaking. "My wife is called Claire."

"Claire?" Mrs Henderson blinked. "But what about Jasmine? You two were so in love! Chris always said—"

"Jasmine died that night. The same night as Chris did. Do you remember, Mrs Henderson?"

It was an effort for Tom to get the words out, but they had to be spoken. Whatever daydream the old lady was lost in, he couldn't share it, no matter how badly he wanted to.

"Oh... Oh, yes, of course." Mrs Henderson shook her head with a little frown as though she was waking up. "I haven't met Claire, have I? Or did you bring her last time you visited? I can't quite remember..."

Tom's heart sank even further. His mother had told him that Mrs Henderson had been forgetful these last few months, but he had no idea it had got so bad.

She'll need to move to a care home soon, he thought to himself. *God knows what'll happen to all these cats when she does.*

As though reading his mind, Mrs Henderson said, "I don't have long left to go, Tom. I can feel myself slipping away just a little bit more every day. Don't look so worried, it's a gentle thing, like drifting off to sleep, except over months instead of minutes."

Tom was surprised by how lucid she suddenly sounded. That was the cruelty of age – Maggie Henderson was continually waking from pleasant dreams of the past to remember with crushing clarity just how much she'd lost. It must keep the pain so fresh in her mind it was like being mentally cut a hundred times every day. He knew she was calling the jarring process of forgetting and remembering gentle for his sake to ease his concern about her. He doubted he could ever be that generous. It was one more thing to add to his long list of reasons for self-loathing.

"I think now's the time for you to have something that belonged to Chris," she said, getting up and shuffling over to a desk by the grimy window. She opened a drawer and rummaged inside, pulling something from under a pile of papers and holding it out to Tom.

It was a leatherbound notebook, with a small padlock that looked like it had been prised open many years ago. Tom turned the book over in his hands, his heart thumping painfully in his chest. Chris had always wanted to be a writer. While the other boys had kicked balls about in the school yard and played war games in the concrete squares of the estate, Chris had sat quietly reading or scribbling notes in one of his many notebooks. He hadn't let Tom read anything he'd written since that time when they were twelve and Chris had showed him a story he'd been working on for months. It had been a silly piece of fluff about aliens invading their town and setting up camp in the local supermarket which ended up blasting off into space, but Chris was proud that he'd managed to finish his first proper story and was eager for Tom's approval.

Tom hadn't given it to him. Instead, he'd laughed and told him it was the dumbest thing he'd ever read. He'd even told a couple of boys at school about Chris's space-supermarket scribblings, and the other kids had called Chris the 'supermarket space cadet' ever since. Tom bitterly regretted it then, but even more so now. Chris had forgiven him – they *had* been best friends after all. But he'd never shown Tom another one of his stories.

"Um, I'm not sure Chris would have wanted me to read this, Mrs Henderson," he said, trying to hand the notebook back. "He was very private about his writing."

"I know he was, but I *know* he would have wanted you to read this. Please, Tom, take a look at it. It'll help you to understand things. Things Chris would have struggled to explain. You two were best friends, but there are things I don't think you fully understood when you were both young. Things he would have wanted you to know."

Ah, but I do know, Mrs Henderson, Tom thought to himself, the image of the two guilty faces flashing through his head. Just before they'd turned to stare at the car roaring towards them, they'd been locked in an embrace. Tom knew all of Chris's secrets. He didn't need to read Chris's story about aliens and outer space to know what was going on in his head the night he'd died.

But Mrs Henderson was insistent, and Tom put the book into one of the empty shopping bags, making a big show of taking it home with him to keep her happy.

Mrs Henderson didn't have long to live. With his parents coming home from Spain at the end of the week, there was a good chance he wouldn't see her again before she was either admitted to a care home, or to the sprawling cemetery near the motorway bypass. There was no more room in the small graveyard up by Gilligan's Park where Chris and Jasmine had been buried twenty-five years ago. There would be no reunion for Mrs Henderson – even in death she'd be divided from her long-lost son.

The thought was a depressing one, and he struggled to summon a parting smile as he hesitated on Mrs Henderson's doorstep.

"You'll be alright till my Mum and Dad get back at the end of the week, won't you?" he asked. "You've got my number beside the phone, so call if you need help with anything before then."

"Oh." Mrs Henderson looked suddenly sad. "You're not coming back this week, then?"

"Um..." Tom tried to think of an excuse. It was bad enough that his parents refused to leave the estate they'd called home for so long and he had to return occasionally to visit them. The last thing he wanted was for Mrs Henderson to guilt-trip him into also visiting her apartment filled with painful memories whenever he was here. "Work's really busy at the moment, so—" he began.

"But you'll be working here on the estate this week, won't you?" Mrs Henderson said with that sudden lucidity that had thrown him before.

"How did you know that?" he asked. "I only saw the duty roster yesterday."

"Oh, the sign's been up for weeks!" Mrs Henderson told him. "They always put those 'work starting here on such-and-such-a-date' signs up ages before anyone actually turns up to work on a road. And there hasn't been any work done on that pot-holed mess of a road for so long, it's caused quite a stir around here to know the council have finally listened to all the complaints."

"Ah." Tom said. He really didn't have any excuse now. "Well, I'll try to pop in one evening after my shift. As long as we don't finish too late," he added, keen to give himself a get-out clause.

"You do that. We can discuss what Chris wrote in his book. I know you'll probably have questions," Mrs Henderson said, giving his hand a motherly squeeze before she closed the door.

Tom stood in the hallway for a long moment, staring at the bag in his hand that contained the unwanted book no doubt stuffed full of secrets he'd found out about years ago. There wasn't anything he could learn about the past that he didn't already know.

He was the one with secrets. Not his dead best friend.

*

Tom was wrong. The past held secrets that were yet to be unearthed, but he only discovered them when work started on the Red Road.

The sun was already warming the horizon when he drove first to the council construction office to collect his work gear and instructions, and then to the Burnback Estate to park down by the tower blocks. He had no choice but to come by the main road this time.

The *Red* Road.

Some folk on the estate said it was called that because there'd been a pub there until the sixties called the Red Rover, others said it was just a random choice, like Blackheath Lane and White Street in town.

Whatever the reason for naming it, the road *had* been red that night.

Tom had seen the blood shimmering in the glow of his car's rear lights when he'd clambered out on trembling legs to inspect the damage. Jasmine's face – beautiful and pale with shock only moments before – had been crushed to a pulp, her head smashed like a pumpkin under the car's heavy wheels. Chris's face had been torn to pieces. His arm had caught on the car's undercarriage and he'd been dragged face down the full fifteen metres it had taken Tom to skid to a stop.

Chris was still alive when Tom had leaned over him.

His nose and lips had been torn off and his eyes had been gouged out by the force of friction across the pot-holed concrete, but he'd known who was there. He'd opened his bloody mouth and gasped—

"Tom, what are you standing there gawping for? Get out of the way of the low loader!"

Tom looked up, blinking in the morning sunlight. He felt like he'd been in a dream since he'd left the construction office. He'd been vaguely aware of gripping the wheel of his car harder as he'd turned off the main highway and driven down the Red Road to the Burnback Estate for the first time in twenty-five years. Drowning in the flood of memories, he hadn't noticed the maintenance crew assembling there for the day's work. He barely remembered parking his car by the first high-rise building and walking slowly back up the Red Road, staring at the ground and seeing blood in his mind where in reality there was only sunlight glittering off stone chips embedded in the old concrete surface.

He looked up now, blinking when he saw he was standing in the middle of the road, blocking the way of the contractor's low loader that was carrying the machinery they needed for the day's work.

He stepped onto the pavement to let it pass, suppressing a shudder when he realised he'd moved to the exact spot where Chris and Jasmine had been when he'd caught them embracing that night and—

Pull yourself together! Tom told himself, seeing Stan and some of the other guys frowning at him. Right now, they wouldn't suspect him of more than a hangover or a bout of summer flu, but if he wasn't careful, he'd give too much of the past away with his odd behaviour.

He shook himself and strode over to the foreman. "Hey Stan – how come the low loader's only come this morning? I thought the milling work was meant to be done by the contractors last Friday so we'd be ready to sweep the surface and spray the bitumen layer today. That's what it says on the duty sheet, anyhow."

Stan shot him a withering look. "When do we ever get to work by the duty sheet when contractors are involved? Lazy sods gave the council some crap over the phone about 'resource overstretch' and said they'd be delivering the milling machine this morning instead."

"'Resource overstretch'?" Tom frowned. "You mean they double booked their equipment over the weekend and sent it to that fancy new housing estate that's being built on Woodfield Farm?"

"Who do you think pays more to rent this stuff?" Stan muttered, nodding at the heavy machinery being unloaded from the long, flatbed truck. "The Brampton Housing Company, or our poxy council?"

"Figures," Tom sighed. He'd hoped to get the work

over and done with as fast as possible. The duty sheet had a day of sweeping and trimming work, followed by another of spraying bitumen and laying the base course, while the final two days were earmarked for finishing the new surface. Four days, tops. That's what he'd been expecting. Now his crew would have an extra day of standing around watching the contractors get the heavy milling work done while their team had little to do.

"Cheer up, Tommy." One of the crew punched him on the arm and nodded over at the wall by the pavement where some of their other workmates were already sitting. "We're getting paid to watch the contractors piss about while we listen to the radio today. Not bad, eh?"

Tom tried to smile back, but for the first time, the thought of a whole day doing very little left him feeling sick. He'd wanted to lose himself in work. He needed to be able to focus his full attention on the job to stop his mind wandering away down dangerous paths to the past. None of his workmates knew about his connection to the Red Road, or what had happened here twenty-five years ago. And he wanted it to stay that way.

That meant putting on a brave face and pretending everything was just fine.

He sat down on the wall with Jim and Alex, taking

the cup of coffee he was offered from a flask and watching the contractors setting up their milling machine. He'd completed his training years ago on the heavy-duty cold planer that chewed up the old asphalt, ground it down and spat it out through the long funnel into the truck driving slowly ahead of it. But it was a boring job, and one that he didn't mind the council outsourcing to the contractors who owned the expensive equipment. He preferred the smaller jobs – the trimming work with a pneumatic drill and the careful sweeping to ensure all the debris from the old layer was removed. He liked things he could concentrate on himself for hours at a time that didn't require him to constantly talk with his colleagues or engage in the juvenile joking and endless innuendo he found so tedious.

It wasn't that Tom was antisocial or didn't like people. He just didn't like that certain way in which people who grew up on estates like Burnback communicated. The gratuitous insults masquerading as friendly banter had always felt hostile, and the constant stream of smut that made up the majority of teenage boys' communication left a sour aftertaste on his tongue. He wanted better conversations – a *deeper* connection, a sense that what was being said actually *mattered*

That's why he'd always got on so well with Chris.

Chris hadn't talked like anyone else he'd ever met on the estate. When he was just a little kid in their first years of school, he'd talked about space exploration and dinosaurs and strange creatures found in the deep sea. A few years later, he was fascinated by thoughts of an alien invasion, discovering Atlantis, and the possibility of a nuclear apocalypse. By the time they'd reached secondary school, and the other pimpled boys were hanging out behind the bike sheds smoking their first cigarettes and discussing female body parts, Chris was knee-deep in politics, philosophy and the books he said changed the world.

That was what Chris wanted to do – change the world with the novels he planned to write. Tom still wished he hadn't laughed at that first story he'd been shown all those years ago. He'd spoiled his chances of reading Chris's more mature work, and it had created a small but discernible crack in their friendship that had never quite healed.

It was Jasmine, though, who'd blown their friendship wide apart. Jasmine with her black hair and those red lips every boy on the estate wanted to kiss. The only time Tom had ever seen real anger in Chris's eyes had been the night he'd come running home from the youth club to tell his best friend that Jasmine Harris had finally let him kiss her. Tom hadn't realised Chris might be harbouring feelings for her too. He'd never seemed to take much notice of the girls at school or around the estate before. But when Tom saw that look on his best friend's face, he'd recognised the green-eyed monster rearing its ugly head.

He'd thought Chris would get over it after a few months. But the longer Tom's relationship with Jasmine went on, the more Chris seemed to resent it, until it became like a festering wound between them. It wasn't until that night on the Red Road, when Tom was driving his father's battered Ford Escort home after helping a couple of local boys shift some stolen goods, that he found out the wound cut both ways.

It still hurt. After all these years, he could still feel the sharp sting of betrayal under the deeper heartache that his own actions had caused.

I shouldn't think about the past, Tom reminded himself again. But it was impossible not to. He was sitting on the wall by the very spot it had happened, and the song playing on Jim's radio was the very one that had been playing on the car's crackly radio when Tom had turned down the Red Road that night and seen—

"Do you want to go deaf, mate?" Jim nudged him in the ribs, clearly irritated that Tom hadn't responded to his attempts to get his attention. "Stick these on – the cold planer's about to start up."

Tom took the ear defenders his colleague offered him,

glad to shut the song out along with the roar of the milling machine as the rotating drum crunched through the top layer of asphalt and ground it into small pieces that were spat out of the discharge conveyor into the dump truck in front. He tried to focus on other thoughts as muffled sounds of scraping and grinding reached his ears through the thick padding – cheerful thoughts about Hannah's upcoming birthday party and the holiday his parents were on. But something was nagging away at the back of his mind, refusing to let him escape the memories of the past.

It took him a long moment to realise he could still hear the song on the radio.

It wasn't tinny and distant, swamped by the far louder churning and thudding of heavy machinery. It was sharp and clear, as though it was being broadcast directly into his head.

Tom glanced at the radio sitting on the wall. Jim had turned it off. The familiar words of the song, however, rang louder and louder in his ears.

'We were only seventeen –
You were sweet and I was mean.
I got lost and then I found
Too late –
Emptiness without you around.'

The song had been playing non-stop on the radio that November. Jasmine had loved it, hoping it stayed number one for three more weeks so it could be her seventeenth birthday song. Tom had secretly hated it – pop wasn't his thing, but he'd pretended to like it for her sake. It had been playing on the radio that night. The night he'd borrowed his dad's car without permission and sneaked out on that job. It had been playing when he'd turned down the Red Road and saw—

Tom blinked. The red he thought he saw in his mind's eye was real, just like the song that was no longer coming from the radio, but was filling his ears none the less. The red was coming from the road before him.

The milling machine was slowly scraping up the dark grey surface of the road, chewing the old asphalt into little pieces and spitting them out of the discharge conveyor into the dump truck ahead of it. But what was coming out of the funnel wasn't bits of ground-up concrete. What was coming out was blood and bone and body parts.

What the..?

Tom gazed in horror at the stream of gore spurting from the long conveyor funnel and spraying into the truck. The song suddenly screamed in his ears, as though the volume on a ghost radio had been cranked up to full.

'We were only seventeen –
You were sweet and I was mean.'

Tom tore off his ear defenders and threw them on the ground, the roar of the milling machine finally drowning out the terrible truth of the old song's lyrics. Without stopping to think what he was doing, he raced to the cab of the slow-moving machine, jumping up and banging on the side to tell the driver to stop. The young worker turned to shout down at him, the startled look on his face signalling loud and clear that he thought Tom was crazy.

Tom didn't wait for the cold planer to stop. He ran to the truck up ahead, clambering up the side to stare into the dump box. It was half full of ground-up asphalt, another load rumbling down the conveyor funnel from the milling machine before the driver had a chance to turn off the engine.

There was no blood in the bed of the dump truck. No white bone and no red gore. There was just the dark grey of concrete against the dull steel of the containment box.

Tom was too confused to work out exactly what happened next. He felt himself being pulled from the side of the truck, but he only realised that Stan was yelling at him when his ears stopped ringing and the foreman's words finally cut through the after-hum.

"...think you're doing?" Stan was yelling. "Are you crazy? You know better than to go anywhere near the machines while they're moving! And why the hell did you take these off?" he waved the ear defenders Tom had dropped and shoved them back into his hands. "You want to lose your hearing, huh? Or are you just trying to drown me in paperwork if you get yourself hurt?"

Tom felt himself swaying, the ground unsteady beneath his feet despite the rumbling machinery now sitting still and silent

"I thought I saw..." Tom trailed off, seeing the other workers all staring at him. He couldn't bear the questioning look in their eyes. The last thing he wanted was to be standing in the Red Road with an audience of suspicious onlookers trying to uncover his terrible secret.

"Sorry, Stan, it won't happen again. I'm going to take a breather and head down to the shops, OK? Does anyone want anything while I'm there?"

Tom tried to act nonchalant as he took orders for bags of crisps and chocolate bars from the rest of the crew. As long as he kept his head, they'd shrug it off as a one-off mistake. They wouldn't question his reasons or his sanity too closely.

Those questions would be left to Tom to figure out. As he walked away down the Red Road towards the Burnback Estate, the images flashed through his mind again. Blood. Bone. Gore. He'd seen the carnage he'd left behind in the tail lights of his father's car as he sped off into the dark that night, but in his mind, the pictures were crystal clear – the burst melon of Jasmine's head melting into the raw meat of Chris's face and everything all mixed up in the present day with the bloody churn of body parts spurting from the milling machine's conveyor funnel.

Tom managed to keep going until he turned the corner by the first tower block and was finally out of sight of the crew working on the road. Leaning up against a wall, he dry heaved for three full minutes before he was able to catch his breath.

He'd known going back to the Red Road would be hard. But if he'd known it would be *this* hard, he would've taken the week off.

Maybe I should just call in sick, he thought. But he'd used up all his paid leave for the year already. He'd had a bout of sciatica in February that had laid him up for two weeks, and he'd had to use all his holiday time in April when Claire's father had a stroke and had to be moved into the care home. If he took time off now, it would be unpaid. And with Hannah's lavish birthday party coming up, that simply wasn't an option. His wife's handmade card business was little more than an expensive hobby despite her claims that she was turning a profit, but he didn't want to upset Claire by asking her to cut back on all the craft supplies she was forever cluttering up the house with.

Just get a grip! he told himself, glancing round to make sure no one was looking his way. A man with a mean-looking pit bull straining on a leash was heading for the small newsagent at the corner of the nearest building. He threw Tom a searching look as he passed. Tom decided to wait till the coast was clear before going to the shop himself to collect the snack orders.

His car was parked by the first tower block, and he climbed back inside to wait for a few minutes out of sight. He wasn't needed on the job today. That meant he'd have about half an hour of breaktime until Stan decided he was taking the piss.

Should I go up and visit Mrs Henderson again like I promised? he wondered.

But the thought of looking the old lady in the eye and commiserating with her about the death that he'd caused all those years ago was more than he could bear right now.

Besides, he hadn't taken a look at Chris's book yet. It was still sitting in a bag on the back seat.

Tom leaned over and retrieved it. Maybe all the weird stuff he'd been seeing and hearing this week had just been his guilty conscience hijacking his rational mind. Maybe reading some of Chris's stories would help him reconnect with the best friend he'd lost, and go some way to making amends for what he did to Chris that night.

It was worth a try.

But when Tom opened up the leatherbound notebook, he found it wasn't full of the short stories he'd been expecting.

It was a diary, and clearly one of a series, as the entry on the first page was dated November 11th – one week before the events on the Red Road.

Tom leaned back in his seat and began to read.

School was shit today. Mr Roberts is off sick for a week, so we got that wanker replacement English teacher again. The guy's so thick he keeps getting 'Hamlet' mixed up with 'A Midsummer Night's Dream'. How are we meant to pass our exams if we're getting taught by this dole-queue dropout that Hamlet's father was some fairy called Oberon and Titania was queen of fucking Denmark?

What a complete toss-pot.

Tom couldn't help grinning when he read that. Trust Chris to think the worst thing that could happen to him at school was having teachers who didn't live up to his high standards. Everyone else had been scared of getting jumped behind the bike sheds or having their heads flushed down the toilets by the football jocks, but Chris's worst nightmare was having a temporary teacher for a week who didn't know one Shakespeare play from another.

Tom stopped smiling when he read the next bit, though.

Really going to have to talk with Tom about Jasmine. They had their faces glued to each other in the canteen all through lunch. I don't think I can take it anymore. It's got to the point where I feel so guilty for hiding my secret from him, I can barely look Tom in the eye. I just don't know how to tell him, though. What if he gets so mad he never speaks to me again? Anything would be better than losing him as my best mate, even putting up with him sucking the face off Jasmine in front of me and the whole of the senior year.

Tom closed his eyes briefly. So it had been going on behind his back for at least a week before that night on the Red Road. Exactly how long, he'd probably never know, not unless Mrs Henderson had a whole stack of diaries hidden away that detailed everything prior to that entry. Tom doubted it, though. Chris had a habit of burning old stories he wasn't proud of – work he'd pretentiously called his 'juvenilia'. He'd probably done exactly the same thing to all his old diaries. This must have been the sole survivor because Chris had never got the chance to finish it. He'd died before his last entries could go on the fire like the rest.

Tom had to force himself to read on. He didn't really want to know the sordid details of Chris and Jasmine's fling behind his back, but this was his chance to relieve a little part of his guilt at what he did. If he could find a passage where Chris spelled out in black and white that he'd been cheating with Tom's girlfriend, then Tom might be able to justify the jealous rage he'd felt. He couldn't be held responsible for losing control when the love of his life had her arms around his best friend, could he?

Eager for absolution, he read on.

But I'm not going to whine about that tonight. It's late, I'm knackered, and I still haven't finished that history essay on Peterloo and the bloody boring Corn Laws. I didn't get much sleep last night. I had that weird dream again, but this time it was more vivid.

I was standing on the Red Road at the edge of the estate, and it was pitch dark. I couldn't see anything except a faint scarlet glow in the distance. There was something wrapping itself around my ankles, and when I looked down, I saw it was a black cat. Except in the dream, I knew the cat was Jasmine – must've been the bright green eyes or something. The cat looked terrified. Anyway, the red glow got closer and closer, until I could see two big eyes coming at me like they were headlamps in the face of some shadowy giant. And just like I knew the cat was Jasmine, I knew the shadowy giant with the red eyes was Tom.

Now this is the freaky bit – the Tom/giant thing opened its mouth, and this time I heard what it said. It was a kind of metallic roar, that sounded like:

'The night was dark as the traitor's heart
on the red, red road.
His eyes turned green at the things he'd seen
on the red, red road.
His temper flared, his prey ensnared,
War declared and a grave prepared,
A sudden blow and blood did flow
down the red, red road.'

I mean, how weird is that??? I've got ideas for stories from dreams before, but not poems. Maybe the universe is trying to tell me that Calliope's my real muse instead of Arthur C. Clarke.

Anyway, really hope I don't have the nightmare again tonight, cos I could really use a decent night's sleep before that maths test tomorrow.

Tom turned the page, his heart pounding. The entry had ended, the next one dated a few days later. He was just about to read that too, when there was a loud knock on the car window next to his head.

"Hey, Tom – are you alright, mate?"

Jim was leaning down and gazing at him in concern. Tom realised the hands that held the book were shaking. He shoved it back in the bag before Jim could get a look at it.

"Yeah, fine, just skivving off for a bit. Stan's not mad, is he?"

"Not yet, but he will be if you don't get back with his cheesy Wotsits in five minutes. The other guys will wonder where their munchies have got to as well if you don't get a move on."

Tom nodded, grateful for the warning, and hurried over to the newsagents to pick up the snacks he'd promised. His head was buzzing, and not just from the aftereffects of pulling off his ear defenders while the milling machine was still operating. Now the sound that whispered in his ears wasn't the song that had played on the radio, but the poem in Chris's diary.

Tom had a horrible feeling that the Red Road had more secrets to reveal, and skinning off the top layer of asphalt was the beginning of a process that would unearth skeletons that were better kept buried.

*

Danny got home late again from the warehouse that evening. Hannah, clearly deciding she didn't want a repeat of the 'you're the golden child and Dad's happy to blow the family fortune on your party' argument, had taken herself off to a friend's house for the night. Tom couldn't blame her. He'd been bracing himself all through dinner for another fight, but when his son finally sat down, perspiring and out of breath from the long walk, he seemed surprisingly sanguine about the state of the bus service. Tucking into his chicken fillets as Tom and Claire were starting their pudding, he talked of hopes of a pay rise come August, and rumours that the shift manager had been stealing some of the more expensive products and selling them at the local market.

Tom made sure to smile at the first piece of news – even if it meant Danny saving up for a car even sooner – and to frown at the second piece of news, even if it made him a hypocrite. He'd never told Claire or his kids about some of the shady activities he'd got up to with the boys from the Burnback Estate when he was Danny's age. He wanted those youthful misdeeds to stay firmly where they belonged – in the past, buried alongside his unforgivable sin.

Claire seemed hell-bent on reopening old wounds.

Whether her refusal to see Tom's point of view was down to the sort of bovine insensibility that sets in after twenty years of marriage, or a more calculated attempt to manufacture drama to spice up their evening meal, Claire just would not let the topic go.

"That's great news about the pay-rise, Danny," she beamed through a mouthful of custard. "You'll have your own little second-hand motor in no time. You might even have it in time for the new school term. The girls will like that."

Claire caught the worried look that Danny shot at his father, and her face hardened. "You're seventeen, Danny – you'll be eighteen before the end of the year. You're legally old enough to buy your own car and drive it regardless of what anyone else thinks."

"Not while he's living under my roof, he he isn't," Tom said darkly. He hadn't meant it to sound like an ultimatum. He'd just had such a long day, he couldn't cope with this again, not tonight. His words hung ominously in the air, draining the warmth from their previously snug kitchen.

Danny set down his knife and fork with a clunk. For a moment, Tom thought he was going to storm off again. But then he did something unexpected. He looked his father straight in the eye and said calmly, "It's not that I don't respect you, Dad. But I'm nearly eighteen, and the 'You can't do something completely normal just because I'm you father and I say so' rule is not going to cut it anymore. Give me one good reason – and I mean a really good, *rational* reason for not letting me buy my own car, and I'll be willing to listen."

That took the wind out of Tom's sails. Tantrums and incoherent teenage rage he could weather. But cold logic was much harder to counter, especially when Danny had finally exposed the shaky foundations his father's flimsy argument was resting on.

Tom put his pudding spoon down and cleared his throat.

What came out next wasn't what he expected. He'd been ready to rehash his previously undercooked reasoning. But suddenly he found himself telling the truth – at least, as much of the truth as he could without exposing the secret that had been eating away at his soul in the small hours of every morning for the last twenty-five years.

"When I was your age," he sighed, "my father didn't allow me to drive either."

"So you know just how frustrating it is, then!" Danny said triumphantly. Seeing the small frown on Tom's face and realising he might be jeopardising the moment of candour, he leaned back and let his father finish.

"Like you, I didn't listen," he continued. "I knew better – we all do when we're teenagers. I saved up for lessons just like you did and passed my test, but your grandad dug his heels in and wouldn't let me borrow his car. He said he needed it for work and he couldn't afford anything happening to it, but I knew he just didn't want me driving it."

Danny managed to keep his mouth shut despite his face betraying an overwhelming urge to shout, 'Then you know how angry I am right now!'. Even Claire managed to bite her tongue to let her husband finish, which was even more of a miracle.

"Son, it's not that I don't trust you," Tom said, "but I know how easy it is to think you know everything in your teens. I thought I knew better than my dad, too. That's why I used to take his car without asking in the evenings, when he was down at the pub."

Danny exchanged glances with his mother. The blank look on her face told him that she'd never heard this story either.

"The thing about being behind the wheel of a car when your brain's not fully matured, is that it makes you feel invincible. You think you can do anything. And worse, it makes you feel like you have a *right* to do anything," Tom said darkly.

"Like what?" Danny said, starting to sound a little doubtful, as though he wasn't sure he really wanted to hear the rest of his father's story.

"Like going too fast," Tom said. "Like showing off to

your mates. Like thinking just because you're young, alcohol won't affect your judgement when you get behind the wheel."

"You mean you were caught drinking and—"

"No, not me," Tom said quickly. He stared at the tablecloth, making sure he picked his words carefully. "But plenty of other kids my age were. I got lucky. One dark November night I took my dad's car and drove around with some mates. We weren't doing anything wrong," he hastened to add, "just bored teenagers with nothing else to do. Before my dad got home from the pub and saw the car gone, I dropped them off on the other side of town."

Tom stared harder at the white tablecloth, concentrating to make sure he didn't trip up and tell the real story – that they'd broken into a house in the upmarket end of town, stolen everything they could get their hands on, then Tom had dropped the boys off at the warehouses down by the flea market where they could offload the TVs and stereo system they'd jacked. Tom had left them to it, trusting he'd get the promised extra cut for taking the most risk as the getaway driver. Those details weren't important now. He'd left that version of himself behind in the past. He was a changed man these days – a loving husband and a responsible father living in a nice neghbourhood.

He tried not to think about the fact that he was now

living in a house very like the one he'd helped to burgle that night.

"It was when I was coming home that I saw it. I wasn't far from the Burnback Estate. There was a car speeding on the wrong side of the road. There was a teenager behind the wheel – a boy my own age. I didn't get a good look at him before he ran me off the road and right into a wall. I burst my nose and cracked two ribs off the steering wheel – we didn't have airbags back then, but that wasn't the worst of it."

"There was something worse?" Claire gasped, half horrified and half outraged that she hadn't been told this story despite how long she'd been married to Tom.

Tom shook his head. "The worst of it was, I wasn't the first person that kid had injured that night. He'd driven up from the Burnback Estate, and hit two people on the Red Road. He killed them almost instantly. Their injuries were terrible."

Tom paused, his eyes stinging from the effort not to blink. He kept them fixed on the white tablecloth, terrified if he looked up he'd catch sight of something red and his mind would spiral into madness the way it had when the milling machine had torn off the top layer of the Red Road that morning.

Danny and Claire sat waiting with bated breath for the end of the story.

"My girlfriend and my best mate were both killed that

night by a kid who thought he had the right to drive a death machine just because the law said seventeen was old enough," Tom said angrily. It was only a half truth. *He* had been that kid, but for the sake of his own sanity, he projected the spectre of death onto a shadowy figure he could hide behind. "I was almost killed myself when he ran me off the road," he added.

That was another half truth. After running over Chris and Jasmine, Tom had turned the car, screeched away up the Red Road, and driven the Ford Escort into a wall at a suitable distance that wouldn't put him right next to the crime scene, but close enough that he could claim to have been run off the road by the same maniac who had killed his friends. They didn't have much in the way of forensic crime budgets back then, and the police certainly weren't going to waste good money on an obvious hit and run in a crappy, rundown estate. They'd swallowed his story when they came across him crying and bleeding over the steering wheel of the smashed-up Escort early the next morning after he'd spent hours crawling under the car with a torch to remove all the bits of blood and bone that could tie him to the nearby crime scene. They hadn't even noticed the odd discrepancy in their official report of a car hitting two people while driving *from* the estate, when the evidence of the tyre marks showed they'd clearly been run over by a car heading *towards* the estate.

There was a deathly silence in the kitchen.

Tom finally risked looking up. He saw the same expression in his son's and his wife's eyes as he'd seen in the eyes of the two policemen who'd found him. Concern, yes, but also the faintest hint of disgust at how vulnerable he looked.

It was his son who broke the silence. "I'm really sorry, Dad," he said, fiddling awkwardly with his fork. "Did they catch the guy who did it?"

Tom shook his head. "The culprit was never caught." That much was true, at least. He let the silence linger a little longer, then added, "So you see, son, why you shouldn't be driving at your age?"

If Tom thought his trump card was a winner, he'd badly miscalculated.

Danny frowned. "Look, I know it must've been terrible losing your best friend and girlfriend to an irresponsible driver, but what's that got to do with me?" The defensive note was back in his voice, the sympathy evaporating from his gaze, replaced with the flash of resentment that Tom was only too familiar with.

"You wanted a good argument!" Tom protested. "Are you seriously saying that two kids losing their lives and me almost losing mine at your age isn't a good reason to ask you to wait until you're older to drive?"

"Are you seriously suggesting that I'm as irresponsible as that drunk kid? Or as irresponsible as you were at my age? " Danny shot back. "You stole your dad's car and went joyriding! I'd never do anything that idiotic!"

"Danny's right," Claire said, taking up her own pudding spoon again and finishing off the custard and sponge cake that was now turning to lukewarm sludge in her bowl. "He's a very responsible young man. He's worked hard to earn his driving lesson money, and he's working even harder to save up for a car. He's more than proved he's responsible enough to drive one."

"*He* might be!" Tom protested, returning to his weakest argument now that his strongest one had backfired so spectacularly. "But my point is, the other drivers on the road aren't."

"Drivers like you, you mean?" Danny said pointedly. Tom opened his mouth to protest, then shut it again when he realised he was out of ammunition. He just couldn't make Danny see the danger that other drivers posed. Not unless he admitted that his son was right – it was drivers like his own father who made the roads into deathtraps for the young. He couldn't bear the thought of Danny's promising young life ending the way that Chris and Jasmine's had – crushed beneath the unforgiving wheels of a vehicle fuelled by jealous teenage rage.

"You said the police never caught the driver of the other car," Danny said, picking up his knife and fork and cutting into his chicken fillet. "So how come you know it was a guy the same age as you?"

"I saw him coming at me," Tom said, his eyes strangely transfixed by the sight of the knife that sawed against the overcooked fillet.

"But you said it was a dark November night, so you would both have had your headlights on, yeah? If he was coming at you on the same side of the road with his headlights dazzling you, how did you get a good enough look at him to see..."

Danny's words seemed to fade away, replaced by the song playing on the radio in his mind. Strangely, the lyrics weren't the ones that Jasmine used to belt out at breaktime in the common room, but the ominous words of the poem that Chris had written down.

'The night was dark as the traitor's heart
on the red, red road...
A sudden blow and blood did flow
down the red, red road...

The chicken breadcrumbs separated like a layer of asphalt under a milling machine, Danny's knife cutting through the white breast and exposing the red blood that ran across his plate and spilled onto the white tablecloth in exactly the same way that Chris and Jasmine's blood had spilled down the red, Red Road and—

"Tom, are you alright, love?" Claire asked, patting his hand. "I know you feel strongly about this, but Danny is an adult now, or as good as. He has to make his own decisions."

Tom turned to look at his wife, but her face seemed to have exploded, blood running down her chin from the bottom jaw that dangled on pieces of gristle from her exposed skull.

"Tom, love?"

Tom blinked. Claire was dabbing at her chin with her napkin, wiping off the white cream and red jam that had spilled over her lips. Her head hadn't burst like Jasmine's had, and Danny's plate wasn't overflowing with blood. It was all in his tired, tortured mind.

"I've had a long day at work," Tom said, getting up too quickly and knocking over the glass of wine by his elbow. It flooded the tablecloth, red as an open artery gushing blood from a fresh wound. He found himself gagging as he raced out of the room and up the stairs, his wife's concerned voice calling to him the whole time it took him to reach the bathroom and vomit his dinner into the toilet.

*

"Jeez, you look like you've been on a right bender last

night," Jim whistled when he saw Tom's pale face the next morning. "I thought your girl's sweet sixteenth wasn't for a few weeks yet? Did you and Claire book yourself a sneaky little champagne-tasting session last night or something?"

Tom shrugged, too tired to think of a witty reply. "Think I'm coming down with a summer cold," he muttered. "My head's a bit fuzzy."

"Oh. They're the worst," Jim managed to sound both sympathetic and completely bored by the explanation. "Do me a favour and don't pass it on, will you? The missus and me have got a week in Tenerife coming up this Sunday, and I don't want to spend it in bed. Well, I do want to spend it in bed, just not with a cold, if you get what I mean?"

Jim elbowed him in the ribs and roared at his own joke. Tom smiled wearily at the innuendo, cursing the contractors yet again for making them spend an extra day on a job that had already caused him so much misery. At least they'd finished yesterday, taking the heavier machinery away with them on the long loader and leaving Stan's crew to repave the stripped road.

"Christ, look at this mess!" Stan grumbled as he inspected the work from the previous day. "They could've done a basic clean-up at least. This lot will clog the sweeper." He glowered at the rubble that had been left strewn across the road by the contractors. It didn't look any worse to Tom than most of the other jobs they'd worked, but he knew Stan was annoyed at the work stretching until Friday too. Stan liked to knock off early at the weekend while still filling in his full timesheet. None of the members of his crew complained, as long as he turned a blind eye to them shaving an hour or two off their shifts here and there too.

"I'll get started on it," Tom volunteered, eager to get the work done as fast as he could. He'd barely got a wink of sleep last night. Every time he closed his eyes, he'd seen visions of blood running down a dark road, and the summer wind whispering round the house had sounded strangely like the old song on the radio played through a layer of static.

He pulled his ear defenders on and started up the sweeper, fixing his mind on the job at hand and refusing to give in to the urge to run back to his car and drive as far away as he could from this scene of guilt and shame and horror.

Think happy thoughts, he told himself. *Think about Hannah's birthday party and how much she'll enjoy it. Think about the fun Mum and Dad are having on the beach right now. Think about Danny's exam results coming in a few weeks and the celebration we'll have when he gets the grades he deserves. Just don't think about the bones and the body parts you're sweeping up.*

Wait, WHAT?

Tom's eyes widened. In the side mirror, he could clearly see the brushes on the underside of the truck sweeping what looked like bloody limbs into the path of the suction hoses. A fifteen-metre smear of gore and gristle painted the rough concrete behind the machine red, just like the stain Tom had seen in his car's rear lights when he'd stumbled out to examine what was left of his best friend and girlfriend that night. He stifled a cry of horror, shutting off the engine and leaping down to see if the crew member the sweeping machine had torn up could be saved.

"Problem?" Stan snapped, marching over.

"Stan! I'm so sorry, I didn't see him!" Tom gasped.

"See who?"

When Tom bent down to examine the gory remains caught in the brushes, he blinked hard. There were only small chunks of concrete and pieces of loose asphalt beneath the sweeping machine. Glancing back, he saw the road behind the machine was clear, the rough layer of exposed concrete pale grey in the sunlight instead of gleaming red.

"I thought… I thought…" Tom stammered, running a hand across his eyes.

Stan laid a hand on Tom's shoulder. "Do you need a day off, mate?" he asked. His tone was neutral, but the fingers digging into Tom's collarbone signalled the foreman's disapproval. Stan clearly thought that Tom had been drinking the night before and had come in to work hungover. It had only happened a couple of times in the fifteen years Tom had worked for the council, but once was one too many times in Stan's book.

"No, it's just a touch of summer flu, like I said," Tom muttered, straightening up quickly. "I can't afford unpaid time off, Stan – not on top of paying for my parents' holiday and with Hannah's birthday coming up."

The foreman's steely gaze softened slightly. With two failed marriages behind him and five kids to support, he knew how expensive families could be.

"Alright, tell you what – I'll let you take an early lunch. Go and walk it off, or sleep it off in the car, whatever you need. I won't clock-watch as long as you're back on the job this afternoon with a clear head."

"Thanks, Stan."

Tom nodded gratefully and trudged down the road towards the blocks of flats. *I'm tired, that's all,* he told himself, forcing the awful image of bloodied body parts from his mind. *If I can just get some sleep, I'll be alright. I just need to get through the next few days then I never have to see this awful place again.*

He'd parked his car behind the first row of buildings, out of sight of the Red Road. Curling up on the back seat, he tried to find the rest that had eluded him for days, but every time he closed his eyes, he saw red. At first he thought it was just the effect of sunlight shining on his closed eyelids, but when he pulled his high-vis vest over his head to act as a sleep mask, the red he saw with his eyes closed only deepened.

Blood pounded in his ears as he twisted and turned on the back seat, trying to find a comfortable position in the cramped space. Forcing himself to lie still, the pounding only got louder, a drumbeat that reminded Tom of the rhythm of the eerie poem written in Chris's diary.

'The night was dark as the traitor's heart
on the red, red road...
His eyes turned green at the things he'd seen
on the red, red road...'

He could almost hear Chris reciting the lines in time to the beat of accusing syllables. Every detail of those terrible few minutes filled with shock, jealousy, rage, grief and guilt played out behind his closed lids – over and over and over again until Tom thought he was going mad.

The night had been dark in the car's red tail lights, Jasmine's head had been burst-melon red, and Chris's torn body had smeared red gore down the red, Red Road…

"This is ridiculous!" Tom said out loud, sitting up and

trying to force his mind back to his comfortable, normal life in the present, the way a child might pinch themselves to check if they were really awake instead of stuck in a nightmare. He knew what he'd done had been terribly wrong, but hadn't he already paid for his crime with twenty-five long years of guilt?

What more can I do? he thought to himself. He had no way of making amends. He couldn't tell his family. It wasn't just the thought of burdening them with the weight of his secret he feared. He couldn't bear the idea of Claire and Danny and Hannah looking at him with the same loathing and disgust he saw reflected in his own eyes in the bathroom mirror each morning. Owning up and telling the police was out of the question. He'd lose his job, go to prison, destroy his family. He couldn't put them through that.

Asking forgiveness from those he'd hurt most wasn't an option either. Jasmine's parents were both dead – her father had died in a prison fight when she was ten, and her mother had descended into an alcoholic fog that ended in death a few years after Jasmine died. And as for old Mrs Henderson, the thought of inflicting fresh wounds on that frail old woman whose life had already been consumed by grief and loss was more than Tom could bear.

As he was rubbing his aching head, trying to work out what to do, his eyes fell on the bag that was sitting on the passenger seat. Leaning over, he plucked Chris's diary out. He'd meant to read it last night, but the fraught discussion with Danny had driven all thoughts of it from his mind. Opening it up to the next entry on November 14th, Tom saw that Chris's handwriting was messier, as though his friend had been stressed or upset. He stared at the words on the page, each one making him feel worse than the last.

I can't take it anymore. It's like a weird kind of emotional cancer that's eating me up from the inside. Tom was over at my place last night. We were just hanging out in my room listening to music like we used to, and I don't think he noticed that anything had changed between us. He kept telling me about how he was going to help the Pikeman brothers do a job on Friday night, and I couldn't talk him out of it. He's dead set on buying Jasmine a fancy birthday present for her seventeenth, and this dodgy job is the only way he can get the cash. Even when she's not in the room, it's like Jasmine is sitting between us, whispering in my ear that I have to tell Tom, I HAVE to tell him.

God, I feel like I'm going crazy with lying.

Tom's stomach knotted painfully, but even though he'd

thrown up his dinner the night before and couldn't face breakfast this morning, he knew the cramp wasn't hunger. He knew he was nearing the truth, the confession that would give him an excuse for the terrible things he'd done that night on the Red Road. He just needed Chris to tell him in his own words that he'd been cheating with Tom's girlfriend, and the terrible weight of guilt Tom had been carrying for the past twenty-five years might finally be eased. But what he read next wasn't the confession he'd hoped for.

I wimped out again, though. I was so pissed off with myself that I couldn't sleep for hours after Tom left. When I did, I had that nightmare again – the one with the red-eyed monster and the green-eyed cat and the weird poem that kept repeating over and over in my head. There's probably some deep, Freudian meaning in it all that I'm missing. I'll think about it some more tomorrow and see if I can work it out, but right now I'm falling asleep over my English homework and my essay on Hamlet makes about as much sense as a pile of scrabble letters chucked randomly onto the page. Huh. That temporary teacher will probably give me an A for it. I don't think that wanker can even read.

Tom turned the page, his heart thumping painfully

when he saw there was only one more entry. The rest of the book was blank. The entry was dated November 18th – the night Chris and Jasmine had died. He only had one more chance to find the confession that would ease his guilt over what he did. He had to find it in that last entry, he just had to.

Before Tom could read any further, a shadow passed by the car window. He looked up to see Jim waving to get his attention, his arms full of the snacks and drink cans he'd bought at the shop. He pointed at Tom then indicated silently in the direction of the Red Road. His meaning was clear.

'Get back to work, mate. Your bunk-off time is up.'

Tom reluctantly replaced the book in the bag and got out of the car, resolving to finish the last entry that evening after Claire had gone to bed. Taking a few deep breaths to settle his nerves, he straightened his high-vis vest and followed Jim back to the road where memory met nightmare.

*

Blood oozed in a slow, sticky torrent from the open wound, smelling strangely sweet in the hot evening air. A bloom of red spread over the splayed fingers, hiding the white bone and exposed gristle in a lurid puddle that grew wider and wider the harder his wife squeezed.

"Tom? Did you pick up Hannah's party invitations from the printers like I asked?"

"Hmm?" Tom's eyes refocused, and he realised he'd been staring vacantly at his wife's plate as she squeezed tomato ketchup over the fish and chips she'd insisted on serving on plates to make the takeaway meal more 'civilised'. There was no blood or bone or body parts. They were all in his head.

The visions were getting worse. When Tom had returned to work, he'd been tasked with trimming the jagged edges of churned-up asphalt that had been left along the kerbside by the heavy milling machine. The whole team had their pneumatic drills out, pounding away with their ear defenders on and their eyes fixed on their section of old concrete. None of them saw what Tom saw. None of them saw the blood that fountained from the road when he dug into it with his drill. None of them heard his cry of terror or saw his shaking hands slipping from the handles as the red geyser seeped away through the cracks in the concrete like melting snow. Stan *did* see the mess that Tom made of his section of work and gave him an earful at the end of the shift, but Tom had barely heard it above the pounding of blood in his ears that accompanied the poem that Chris was reading over and over and over in his mind.

"TOM!"

"Hmm? What?"

He finally looked up, the frown on his wife's face warning him that she was on the verge of losing patience with him. He musn't let her suspect there was anything wrong, or else she might sniff out his secrets under the scent of blood and the stench of guilt and the stink of fear that clung to him every moment of every—

"Did you go to the printers today or not?"

Tom clutched his fork hard, willing his mind back to the present. "Sorry, pet. It's been a busy few days. I'll pick them up tomorrow."

"But I wanted to post them tomorrow!" Claire sighed, disappointment vying with irritation for control of her face. Tom had learned to loathe that particular combination over the years. It screwed Claire's mousey face into a pout that was more rodent-like than ever. Jasmine had never looked at him like that. Jasmine's face had been incapable of twisting itself into the ugly, shrewish scowls his wife threw at him across the dinner table. Maybe that was because in his mind, Jasmine's beautiful face was forever seventeen, forever perfect.

Except for that night on the Red Road, when her face had been caved in by the force of the car wheels driving over her head and crushing it into the concrete, of course.

Tom threw down his fork, fighting the urge to gag.

"What is it?" Claire demanded when he jumped up

from the table.

"I need some air. I'm going for a walk."

"Some air?" Claire's peevish voice followed him down the hall. "But you've been working outside all day!"

Tom had intended to wait until Claire was in bed to read the last entry in Chris's diary. But he couldn't stand it any longer. He had to know. He had to find out if those final pages contained the confession of betrayal and the absolution he was searching for. But he didn't make it to his car. When he opened the front door, he was greeted by another car pulling into the driveaway.

The car was red, the same type as the one he'd driven himself that terrible night.

"What the...?"

Tom's eyes widened when he saw his son behind the wheel of the second-hand Ford Escort. Danny stopped the car and stared back at his father, his challenge rumbling like silent thunder through the windshield when he turned the engine off.

'*Your move, Dad.*'

Before Tom could say a word, Claire came hurrying behind him, her shrill tones rising in pitch when she saw Danny climbing out of the newly arrived Ford Escort.

"Danny! You did it! You bought the car you've been saving for!"

There was no condemnation in her voice despite him

going against his father's wishes, only pride.

"Yeah, Derek at work lent me some cash so I didn't miss out on the deal. Not bad, huh?" he said, half pleased with himself and half wary of the strange expression in his father's eyes.

"It's a beauty, isn't it, Tom?" Claire said, nudging her husband in the ribs. She clearly wanted him to accept the fait accompli without further resistance, and for a moment, she thought he'd given in. Tom's silence wasn't evidence of his acceptance, though. He was simply struggling to find his voice amid the torrent of sounds bombarding his mind. His blood was pounding louder and louder in his ears, the rhythmic words of Chris's poem all mixed up with the accusing lyrics of Jasmine's favourite song.

'You were only seventeen on the red, red road.
You were sweet and I was mean
on the red, red road.'

"You can't drive it," Tom finally gasped, his voice barely more than a whisper.

"What?" Danny frowned.

"I said, you CAN'T DRIVE IT!"

This time, Tom's words rang loud and clear down the whole street, and Mrs Potter next door leaned over the hedge where she was watering her geraniums to see what was going on.

Danny shook his head in disbelief. "What the hell is

wrong with you, Dad? You're acting like a loony. I've passed my test and bought a car, and that's the end of it."

"You're not going anywhere in that thing!" Tom lunged for Danny's car keys, but his son was too quick for him. He dodged out of the way, and Tom went sprawling onto the driveway.

"Tom, stop this!" Claire cried, far more appalled at the prospect of the neighbours watching her husband make a scene than the fact he might have hurt himself.

Tom could barely see past the red mist that was clouding his vision. Twisted images of blood and bone and body parts tangled with the imagined horror of his son driving to his death in the same red Ford Escort Tom had driven that awful night. He'd murdered Chris and Jasmine in a jealous rage, and now the universe was going to punish him by forcing him to sit by the phone every night, waiting for a call that would tell him his son had died in some terrible, karmic road accident. He couldn't let it happen, he *couldn't*.

Tom staggered up and stumbled back into the house, heading for the kitchen. He barely heard Danny's footsteps and Claire's concerned questions following him down the hall. He knew what he needed to do. Pulling open the drawer by the sink, he rummaged around until he found what he was looking for.

"Dad, put that down."

Tom whirled round to see Danny standing on the

other side of the kitchen table, his hands raised as though trying to calm a mad dog. Claire was frozen in the doorway, a look of terror on her face.

Hannah had come running down the stairs to see what the fuss was about, her lips growing pale as she peered at him over her mother's shoulder.

"Dad? What are you doing with that?" Her voice was trembling as though she was about to cry.

Tom looked down to see that he was clutching a sharp knife in his hand. What was he doing with a knife? For a moment, it all seemed so confused, and he snatched at the fragments of coherent thought he glimpsed through the red mist in his mind.

"It's OK, pet, I just... I just need to stop Danny driving, that's all."

"With *that*?" Hannah whimpered.

"No. Yes, I mean, it's for the tyres. Just for the tyres."

Danny's eyes had taken on the glassy sheen of disbelief. "You're going to slash the tyres of my car to stop me driving?" he gasped. "Dad, have you *any* idea how fucked up that is?"

The shock of his usually polite son swearing at him finally cut through the fog in Tom's mind. He dropped the knife back in the drawer and shut it quickly. "No, I'm not going to… But you can't, Danny. You can't drive that car."

“I’m done with this shit, Dad. You need help. *Professional* help.”

Danny turned and stomped back down the hall, muttering something to his mother and sister on the way past. Tom thought it sounded something like, ‘If he does it again, call the police’, but the blood was pounding in his ears again and Chris was whispering, whispering, whispering the words of that damn poem, and all Tom could think about was the fact that Danny was heading for the driveway where that red Ford Escort was sitting.

Danny reached the car before Tom caught up with him. Gunning the engine, he reversed out of the driveway and sped off down the road. Tom’s howl of anguish was almost primal.

“Danny! Come back!"

He ran to retrieve his own car keys, almost knocking Claire over in his stampede to reach the pocket of the coat hanging on the rack.

“Tom! Stop! Where are you going?”

“I have to catch up with Danny! I have to make him see the danger he’s in!”

“Dad, stop this, please!”

Hannah was crying now, her shoulders heaving and her body shaking in fright. He knew he must look crazy, but it didn’t matter, nothing mattered except stopping Danny from driving and keeping him safe.

Roaring off down the road in pursuit of the car that had disappeared onto the main road, Tom was barely aware that the radio had turned on of its own accord and was playing a throwback hit list of old classics.

'We were only seventeen –

You were sweet and I was mean...'

*

"Here you go, mate. They were out of cheesy Wotsits, so I had to get you salt and vinegar sticks instead."

Tom's hands were shaking so hard he struggled to open the bag of crisps Jim tossed to him. Alex and his other teammates exchanged glances as they went back to work, but no one asked him any questions. There had been an odd look in Tom's eyes when he'd turned up to work an hour late that morning. A look so wild and strange that even Stan kept his disapproving comments to himself.

Tom sat on the wall, eating the crisps slowly and hardly tasting them. He didn't deserve this extra break – he'd barely worked half the time the others had. But his head was so fuzzy through stress and lack of sleep he couldn't summon the energy to care about how lazy he looked.

He hadn't caught up with Danny's car last night. He'd turned onto the main road too late, and got stuck behind a convoy of cyclists on their evening workout. *That's the problem with living in a middle-class neighbourhood,* Tom thought sourly. *It's full of pretentious aresholes with pretentious hobbies.* Growing up in the Burnback Estate, the only time he'd seen anyone with a bike was when they'd nicked one of the ones padlocked to the stands at the front of the shopping centre near the posh end of town.

Tom had driven around for hours, only giving up when he was nearly out of petrol and he realised he hadn't brought his wallet with him. Returning home, he'd sat on the front steps, waiting and waiting and waiting until Danny finally came home long past midnight. Danny hadn't said a word to his father when he saw him sitting in a pathetic heap in front of the house. He'd just stepped over him and unlocked the door, heading upstairs to bed without a backwards glance. His son's silent condemnation knocked all the fight out of Tom. He'd spent hours planning how he'd slash the tyres of Danny's car, break the windows, cripple the engine – anything to stop his son from driving the damn thing. But when it came to it, he was so tired that all he could do was drag himself to the sofa to lie down.

He'd only intended to rest for a few hours and get up early to make sure Danny didn't drive the car to school. But it was Claire who'd shaken him awake after

Danny and Hannah had left, warning him he was going to be late for work. She didn't suggest he take the day off despite his pale face. She clearly didn't want him in the house.

Tom had got the distinct impression that his wife was afraid of him.

He was running so far behind schedule, he didn't even have time to shower or change his clothes before he stumbled to his car. That was when he noticed that Danny's Ford Escort wasn't in the driveway. He'd taken it to school, and he'd no doubt given Hannah and her friends a lift too.

The thought of both of his children speeding down the road in that death trap made him double up and dry heave.

In the end, it wasn't oversleeping and getting caught in the rush-hour traffic that caused him to miss the first hour of his shift. It was driving to his kids' school and checking the car park to make sure Danny's Ford Escort was there that took him so long. Even that did little to reassure him.

"Planning on getting off your arse at any point today, Tom?"

Stan had dropped all pretence of playing nice and was scowling at him from under his hard hat. Tom threw his half-finished crisps into one of the waste buckets and stood up. "I'll drive the truck with the stone chippings," he offered. "Jim prefers the bitumen sprayer, and Alex likes the roller."

"Fine. But keep your eyes on me and don't start spreading until I tell you to, OK? I don't want you nodding off and driving up Jim's backside," Stan warned.

Tom didn't protest that unlike some of the new trainees who kept screwing up, he'd never done anything that stupid, even when he'd been a newbie himself. After his lame-duck performance over the last few days, his foreman had every right to question his competence.

Jim was already sitting in the bitumen tar sprayer parked at the top of the road by the time Tom reached the truck carrying the stone chips that was parked directly behind it. Despite being nearly fifty, Jim's wide grin gave him the look of a five year old who'd been granted his birthday wish to play in a real workman's truck for the day. Tom usually didn't mind his job, but he'd never have the enthusiasm for it that Jim displayed.

"Let's get some road laid!" Jim called, punching the air like a racing car driver who'd just won the Grand Prix. "You ready back there, kid?" he called. Alex, the youngest member of their team by at least fifteen years, gave a thumbs-up from the cab of the heavy roller-compactor parked at the back of the three-vehicle convoy.

Tom climbed wearily into the truck carrying the stone chippings. By rights, Stan should have been driving it, but he clearly didn't trust Tom with the job of marking off sections to be sprayed and directing the vehicles from the ground. It wasn't taxing, but it did require the operations manager to be awake and alert. Tom could just about manage to drive the stone-chip truck in a straight line when Stan waved him onto the newly sprayed section, and that was about it today.

"Alright, bring her forward," Stan called from up ahead.

Jim started up the bitumen tar sprayer, the red liquid misting the road as the tanker drove to the first bollard Stan had laid out.

Wait.

The *red* liquid?

Tom stared in horror at the road ahead. Instead of the layer of black tar he'd expected to see, the exposed concrete was glistening with blood.

"Tom, you're up!"

Stan banged on the side of his truck impatiently.

"But..."

Tom stared straight ahead at the river of blood flowing down the road. *It should be black*, he told himself in disbelief. *Tar is always black.*

"Tom, what's the problem?"

There was no use asking Stan if he saw black tar or

red blood. He clearly didn't see what Tom could see. And that meant Tom was losing his mind, just like his family feared.

It's tar, just black tar, he told himself as he eased the truck forward slowly, stone chips dropping into the wet bitumen at a steady rate. *Keep your mind on the job. You can get through this, just don't think about that night.*

But his mantra only helped him as long as he stared straight ahead and told himself he was seeing black instead of the red his mind was insisting on. When he reached the back of the sprayer and stepped down from the cab to double check what was really under the truck's tyres, he let out a gasp.

It wasn't stone chippings he'd been spreading onto a surface of newly sprayed tar. He'd been spreading bits of white bone and gristle onto a layer of wet blood.

"No…" he groaned, gazing in horror at the road behind. The roller-compactor was rumbling over the newly laid surface, crushing the pieces of bone into the thick crust of blood that was already starting to harden like a scab over a deep wound. Tom felt his mind reeling as he stared at the terrible sight only he could see.

There was something lying in the middle of the road, just ahead of the roller. It was a face, a beautiful disembodied face that was turned towards him in pleading as the heavy machine rumbled towards it. Tom knew what would happen next, but he couldn't seem to tear his gaze away as the roller ran right over that lovely face with its jade-green eyes, the skull popping like a ripe melon just the way it had when Tom's tyres had driven over it that night. The face was slowly crushed beneath the roller, ground into the road along with the bits of bone that had once been Chris's jaws and arm, and the gristle that had once been his nose and ears.

"Dear God, no!" Tom wailed, stumbling back. He tripped over the edge of the kerb, sprawling onto the pavement and landing in a trembling heap.

"Jesus wept!" Stan snarled, pulling him back onto his feet. "I've let you off these last few days because we're mates, Tom, but if you come to work drunk again, I'm putting you on suspension. Get yourself home in a taxi, and don't report for duty until you've sobered up. And I mean *properly* – see a doctor, get some therapy, whatever it takes. You'll be on unpaid leave till I'm sure you've sworn off the sauce for good."

"But Stan, *look*!"

Tom gestured wildly at the road, but it was no good. It was covered with a layer of fresh, black tar and grey stone chippings, just as it should have been. Jim was leaning out of his cab and Alex was staring through the windows of the roller at him in concern. The rest of the team were standing on the opposite pavement, whispering about him under their breath.

Everyone thought he was mad: his wife, his children, his workmates.

Maybe I am, he thought, slinking back to the tower blocks with his shoulders hunched in shame. *I'm seeing things. Sane people don't see things that aren't there. This is my punishment for what I've done.*

Tom couldn't help throwing his head back and laughing in the same wild-dog-howling-at-the-moon way as Stan when he was amused. But the sound that came out was a bitter growl. He felt certain he wouldn't get let off with such a light sentence. Madness wasn't going to be his only punishment. He knew, deep down, that revenge would come in the form of a car driving the wrong way down a road, turning his world red the way he'd turned his friends inside out and their parents' lives upside down.

"Tom?"

The voice was half hesitant, half fearful. Tom realised his head was still thrown back and he was staring up at the sky with a wild look in his eyes as he crossed the courtyard between the buildings. He turned round to see a woman with a pinched face and skinny arms looking at him suspiciously.

"Sandra. I haven't seen you in a while." It felt strange to be making small talk with one of his parents' neighbours when his whole world was turning red, but nothing had made sense since the moment his feet had found their way back to the Red Road after an absence of twenty-five years.

"Have you been to see Mrs Henderson?" Sandra asked, her arms twitchy under the sweater that was too big for her skinny limbs and too hot for the summer sun. Tom could spot the addicts on the estate from a mile away. They were the ones who always covered up their track marks regardless of the weather. He tried to stop his mind from spiralling down rabbit holes chasing the question of whether his loosening grip on reality had made him look like an alcohol addict to Stan this week, focusing instead on the question he'd been asked.

"Mrs Henderson? Yes, I saw her on Sunday."

"No, I mean today." Sandra shoved one of her twitchy hands into her pocket, fishing for a packet of cigarettes. "She doesn't look good at all. She might need an ambulance."

"Have you called one?"

Sandra shook her head. "Not really my business, is it? But thought you should know, with your mum being pals with her and everything." Having passed on her message, Sandra drifted away aimlessly in the direction of the wasteland, with no more purpose than a leaf on the breeze.

Bloody addicts! Tom thought angrily, rousing himself

properly from his brain fog for the first time in days and marching to his parents' building. No wonder Stan was furious with him. An ill workmate was one thing. An addict workmate was someone who couldn't be relied on. And no matter how much he might want to blame Sandra for not being there for Mrs Henderson, Tom knew he was the one to blame. It was his job to check in on the old woman when his parents were away. He'd said he would. Instead, he'd left her in that pokey little flat all alone with only her army of stray cats for company.

Tom was out of breath by the time he'd climbed to the ninth floor. It took five minutes of hammering on the door and ringing the bell for her to answer. He was ready to put his shoulder to the heavy wood by the time he heard a faint scrabbling from the other side and the door finally opened a crack.

"Mrs Henderson? It's me, Tom Jackson. Are you alright?"

Tom pushed the door the rest of the way, finding the frail old woman standing in the hall in her night-dress and slippers looking confused.

"Tom? Oh, I thought it was Chris. He's late. He said he was going for a walk with Jasmine and he'd be back by ten. It must be nearly midnight by now."

Midnight? Tom frowned to himself. If the old lady couldn't tell midday from the middle of the night, she was in a worse state than he feared.

"Come and sit down, Mrs Henderson," he said soothingly. "I'll make you a cup of tea."

"Thanks, Tom. You're a good boy," the old lady sighed as he helped her onto the sofa. "You didn't see Chris tonight, did you? He never comes back later than he says he will. Maybe I should go and check with Jasmine's mother. Maybe he went back to her place."

Kelly Harper's been dead for twenty-three years, Tom thought. *The Patel family's been living in that flat since then.* He wasn't sure whether to remind the confused old lady of this fact or not. Would it help bring her back to the present? Or would it just frighten her when she realised how mixed up she was?

"Oh, I wish Chris was back!" Mrs Henderson fretted, wringing her bony hands together anxiously. "I'm worried something's happened to him."

Tom felt his guts writhing in guilt. "Let me get you that tea," he said, hurrying to the kitchen to escape from the old woman's distress.

This must have been what she went through that night, he realised. He'd avoided thinking too hard about how the news had been broken to Chris and Jasmine's mothers, focusing instead on the awful hours he'd spent sobbing over the steering wheel after he'd deliberately driven his car into that wall. Now, instead of those hours playing out in his head, he had front-row seats to the quiet drama that had played out in Mrs Henderson's living room as she waited for the police to knock on her door and tell her that her only child was dead.

She must have gone through hell, he thought, glancing over his shoulder at the old woman rocking back and forth on the sofa. *At least Jasmine's mum would have had the comfort of half a bottle of vodka in her system to cushion the blow when the police came knocking.*

He didn't want to think about it. He didn't want to think about Mrs Henderson's anguish or the pain Kelly Harper would have felt when the alcohol haze finally lifted and her loss finally sunk in. He wanted to focus on his own hurt feelings – the betrayal he'd felt when he saw his best friend embracing his girlfriend, the red-hot rage that had given way to grief at his impulsive actions, and the terrible, aching guilt that had plagued him every day for twenty-five years since.

Now, though, there was another overriding feeling that blocked all the pain and guilt out, and that was fear.

Fear that he was losing his mind.

And fear that now he'd broken his own promise to himself and returned to the scene of the Red Road crime, he'd awoken a spirit of vengeance that would not rest until he'd paid in full.

"What the..?"

Tom stopped in dismay at the door of the tiny kitchenette. Cats were on every surface, spitting and snarling at each other as they fought over the mouldy crumbs sticking to the rusting toaster and the remains of days-old instant noodles congealing in a bowl by the sink. The loaf of bread Tom had left on the counter on Sunday had been torn to shreds and devoured, and one cupboard above the countertop was standing open, biscuit packets flayed to pieces and every morsel consumed by the ravenous cats.

Tom braved the claws and bared teeth to sweep a tangle of cats off the counter by the sink and open a cupboard to look inside. The tins of cat food were still on the shelf, unopened. Things really were as bad as Sandra had implied. All Mrs Henderson had left in the world was her cats. If she was so lost in her own thoughts that she'd forgotten to feed them for days, then the end couldn't be far off.

The grim condition of the cramped kitchen was sobering. Tom took charge of the situation with a decisiveness he hadn't felt in days. Picking up several of the cats at a time, he shut some in the bathroom, some in Mrs Henderson's bedroom, and another armful in the hall cupboard. He couldn't face opening the door to Chris's old room. He felt sure Mrs Henderson had left it just the way it had been that night when Chris arranged to meet Jasmine behind Tom's back. He couldn't face seeing the faded film noir posters on the wall or the tall bookcase with the first editions Chris had collected. He didn't want to be reminded of how special Chris had been, and how much more he'd aspired to in a future life lived beyond the confines of the Burnback Estate.

Tom couldn't bear the terrible certainty that Chris would have made something of himself if he'd just been given the chance to grow up. If he hadn't been killed by his best friend at seventeen. If his body hadn't been churned to pieces as it was dragged down a blood-smeared road that night and his wonderful mind smashed to pieces by—

Stop it! Tom ordered himself. *Focus on Mrs Henderson and what she needs right now.*

What the old woman needed was someone to feed her cats before they turned feral and decided her nose and fingers were a more appetising option than starving to death. Tom emptied cans of cat food into bowls and shoved them behind each of the doors the cats were congregated behind, making sure that none of them got out. Leaving them to fight over the food, he turned his attention to making the old woman tea and bringing her a plate of biscuits from the tin the cats couldn't get into.

"Here you go, nice and sweet, just the way you like it," he said, setting the mug down on the cluttered coffee table. He wasn't sure the old lady would be able to lift it. Her hands were shaking so badly it was clear she was in deep distress.

"I think it's time I called an ambulance and got you to the hospital," he said, realising that her problems were much worse than mental confusion, and the situation was beyond saving with tea and biscuits.

"Hospital?" Mrs Henderson gasped, gazing at him with wide eyes. "Why? Has something happened to my Chris?"

Tom sucked in a breath, screwing up his courage for the lie he realised would be the kindest thing at this late stage. "Chris is fine, Mrs Henderson. He's talking to Jasmine outside. I saw them on my way up here. He'll be back soon."

"Oh, thank goodness!" The old woman's tense body finally relaxed and she rested her head against the back of the sofa, her pale lips quivering. "I was so worried! Did you talk with him, Tom? Did you get it all sorted out between you? He didn't think I knew about it, but you can't hide these things from a mother. I knew how he felt, how it was eating him up inside. You don't blame him, do you Tom? He couldn't help it."

Tom's hands clenched reflexively into fists, and he jammed them into the wide pockets of his work trousers. "Yes, Mrs Henderson. Chris told me everything. It's all fine. We've worked it out."

"You're such a good boy, Tom." Mrs Henderson's smile was weak, but the sentiment behind it was so warm Tom felt his heart breaking. He couldn't do this. He couldn't keep lying to the old woman. Maybe her mind was so far gone that she wouldn't understand his confession, but he had to make it now, while he still had the chance.

"Mrs Henderson, I need to tell you something," he stammered, his words catching in his suddenly dry throat. "It's about Chris."

"Yes," Mrs Henderson said, closing her eyes and settling further back into the cushions. "Chris told you, didn't he? You know the secret he was keeping."

"Yes, I do," Tom said, pulling his fists from his pockets again and playing with a biscuit from the plate so that he had somewhere – *anywhere* – to look than the face of the trusting old woman he'd been lying to for twenty-five years. "And... I wasn't honest with you, Mrs Henderson. I got angry when I found out. I was in the car and I saw them together – Chris and Jasmine. I saw them with their arms around each other and I knew they were getting together behind my back. I couldn't take it, I just couldn't! And I… I…"

The biscuit crumbled in Tom's fingers as he fought to control the tidal wave of anger and guilt and grief that coursed through him. He stared at the pieces falling onto the dusty carpet, remembering how his best friend's and his girlfriend's bodies had crumpled under the wheels of his car that night. He had to tell the truth or he'd never be free of those awful memories.

"I was the one who drove the car that night, the car that killed Chris," he said, his voice echoing in the silence as he stared at the ruined mess of biscuit on the floor. "I was the driver. I should have told you before now, but I just couldn't. I'm so, so sorry, Mrs Henderson. Can you ever forgive me?"

Tom waited, his eyes stinging as he continued to stare at the pieces of pink wafer on the grey carpet. There was something eerily familiar about that sight. Something that reminded of him of pink chunks of flesh ground into grey concrete. He shivered at the memory, a chill of foreboding running down his spine.

He looked up.

Mrs Henderson was staring at him with eyes so wide they seemed in danger of popping from her skull, the way that Jasmine's eyes had when his car's tyres had burst her head open. Her face was contorted in shock, her mouth wrenched to one side as though she'd suffered a terrible stroke.

"Mrs Henderson?" Tom gasped.

The old woman didn't blink.

It took Tom a few more heart-stopping moments to realise she was dead.

*

"Tom? The hearse is here. It's time."

Claire had to repeat herself twice through the closed bathroom door before her husband heard. He was sitting on the mat, staring at the open diary in his hands in shock. It couldn't be true. What he'd just read changed everything.

Everything.

"Tom! Are you ready?" Claire added three sharp knocks on the door for emphasis.

"Yes, just a moment!" Tom called. "You go on, I'll be down in a minute."

He drew in a long breath as the sound of Claire's heavy footsteps faded away down the stairs. After what he'd just read, he needed time to compose himself before facing the world again.

He stared at the diary, the words a blur through the tears he was struggling to hold back. He'd been so occupied with making funeral arrangements over the last few days, he hadn't had the mental energy to spend on that last entry. After Mrs Henderson all but confirmed his suspicions with her last words, he hadn't felt the same burning desire to read Chris's confession. But now that he had, he knew that his excuse for his actions twenty-five years ago – his jealously, his *justifable* jealously – was a crutch he could no longer lean on.

The truth was right in front of him in black and white, the truth he would have seen if he'd only looked for it in the cold light of day instead of interpreting the shadows he'd seen though jealous eyes in the car's headlights that night.

Tom wiped away the uncried tears and re-read the last diary entry Chris had ever written.

I'm meeting Jasmine in twenty minutes. I couldn't talk Tom out of doing that job with the Pikeman brothers tonight, and I'm worried sick he'll get caught, but at least it'll give me a chance to talk to Jasmine without Tom being there. I think she'll understand. She's got a gentle side to her, when she's not mouthing off at the boys on the estate or yelling at her mother for drinking their benefits money. I know she won't tell anyone, and I need to offload this secret before I burst. I can't tell Tom, not yet. I don't think he's ready to hear it. What would I say to him? How the hell do you tell your best friend you've been in love with him since you were five years old? How can you drop a bomb like that and not have it blow up in your face?

I know telling Jasmine won't change the fact that I'm caught in this hopeless triangle that I can never square. But she deserves an explanation for how cold

I've been to her. She thinks I don't like her, and that's just not true. She makes Tom happy, and if I can't have him, then I want him to be with someone who makes him smile. God, I'm so nervous at the thought of telling anyone my secret that my hands are shaking writing this. Maybe it's stress from lack of sleep. If I have that bloody dream one more time about the red eyes and the green eyes and the poem that's been going round and round my head, then I'm going to lose my mind. Maybe it's the pressure of bottling up my feelings for so long that's sending me round the bend. Maybe once I've shared my secret I'll feel better.

I hope so.

Right. Time to go – alea iacta est, and all that Latin crap.

Tom closed the diary with a thump. There was no more. That was the last sentence his best friend ever got to write. And it was a fitting one – it was time to go. Time for Tom to go to the funeral of an old woman who'd either died from twenty-five long years of grief, or twenty-five seconds of intense shock. Either way, it was Tom who'd caused her death, just like he'd caused the death of the best friend and girlfriend who'd both loved him.

He hurried back to his bedroom to shove the diary into the bottom of his sock drawer and straighten his tie, then he pulled on his smart jacket and headed downstairs.

The hearse was standing in the driveway, next to Tom's car. Danny's car was gone. The minute Tom had got home after waiting for the ambulance that collected Mrs Henderson's corpse, he'd taken a hammer and a pair of wire cutters to the engine of Danny's Ford Escort. If Tom was lucky, it would rot in the repair shop. Danny hadn't spoken a word to his father for days, but Tom could just about bear the thought of his son's eternal silence if it meant he'd be spared the pain of Danny's eternal death.

There was a part of him that knew his obsession with Danny driving was crazy, that his son was in no more danger on the road than the millions of other drivers up and down the country. But there was a bigger part of him that was convinced a reckoning was due for his own actions, and that punishment would come in the form of his two children being taken from him on the road, the way he'd taken the lives of two teenagers just on the cusp of adulthood.

"Come on, Tom! Hurry up!"

The rear door of the hearse was open, and Claire was waving to him from the back seat. He climbed in, keeping his eyes averted from the coffin stacked with flowers that sat in the long compartment behind them. He already knew what it looked like. He'd spent three hours at the funeral home picking the wood finishings and velvet trims, and hours more at local flower shops choosing the finest bouquets. Mrs Henderson's life had been so small and sad, he couldn't bear the thought of her send-off being anything less than perfect.

Claire saw the way her husband's lip twisted as his eyes slid off the coffin, and as usual, she misinterpreted his thoughts.

"Don't worry," she said, giving his arm a squeeze. "Hannah doesn't blame you for spending her party money on the funeral. She understands this is more important."

Tom tried not to snort. Paying for Hannah's party was the least of his worries right now. Stan had let him have the rest of Thursday and Friday off to deal with Mrs Henderson's funeral arrangements, and he'd been gracious enough not to kick up a fuss when Tom told him he'd have to hold the funeral on the Monday as his parents wouldn't be back from Ibiza until the Sunday night. But there had been hints dropped. Suggestions of no more shifts until a doctor's report could be produced to vouch for Tom's mental health. Tom knew he wouldn't pass in the state he was in. He had to pull himself together.

Maybe laying Mrs Henderson to rest would finally

release him from the purgatory of guilt he'd been living in for the last twenty-five years. He *had* confessed to Mrs Henderson before she died, after all. Surely that counted for something?

Claire kept up a constant stream of small talk with the hearse driver all the way to the Burnback Estate where his parents were waiting to be collected. With no living family, Mrs Henderson's funeral ceremony at the crematorium would be a small affair, and the Jacksons would have to serve as lead mourners. Tom tried not to dwell on the fact that the people representing Mrs Henderson in the hearse and the front row at the ceremony would be: a pensioner who called Mrs Henderson a 'mad old cat lady' when he was feeling uncharitable; another who resented volunteering to do her shopping and cleaning and told neighbours she should be in a care home; a woman who'd never met her; and a man who'd murdered her only son.

"Ugh, I hate this place," Claire suddenly shivered in disgust.

Tom looked up to see they'd reached the turnoff to the Red Road. "You didn't need to come," he snapped, his temper fuelled more by the fear of driving down that awful road again than by irritation at her snobbery.

"And how would that have looked?" Claire shook her head. "People would talk if you went to the funeral alone."

"Who?" Tom said, his voice turning nasty. His heart was pounding as they drove down the newly tarmacked road, his mouth sand-paper dry. Fighting a panic attack, he turned his fear on his wife. "Who would talk? You don't know anyone here. You've visited my parents all of three times since we got married, and you've made them come to our house every other time. You wouldn't even let them babysit their own grandkids, for God's sake! They were never good enough for you. No one from here was. Not even me. I don't know why you even married me in the first—"

Tom's unhinged rant was cut short by a sudden bang and the lurch of the hearse to one side.

"What was that?" Claire cried.

The driver slapped the steering wheel in annoyance. "Damn it! We've hit a pothole. Sounds like it took out the front tyre."

They clambered out to inspect the damage. The front left wheel of the hearse was slowly deflating in a waist-deep crater in the new concrete.

"How the hell did that giant pit get here?" Tom gasped. "We repaired the road just last week!"

"It wasn't exactly a thorough job, was it?" Claire muttered, clearly still smarting from his accusations.

"This road was perfect last time I saw it," Tom insisted. "Unless a bloody bomb went off, I don't see how something this size could have got here."

"It doesn't matter how it got here," the hearse driver grumbled. "The car's stuck so deep I'll need a tow truck to pull it out."

"But what about..." Tom didn't want to say the word *coffin* out loud. He gestured to the back of the hearse instead.

"You know someone with a phone?" the driver asked. "Those new mobile things are too expensive for my boss to pay for, and they're the size of bricks. Doubt I'd get a signal way out here anyway."

"We're picking my parents up from here," Tom said, "you can use their phone." He was kicking himself now for not insisting they wait for the hearse at the top of the Red Road where it joined the main street. His parents had said it was only right to drive down to the estate with the coffin to give any last-minute well-wishers a chance to say goodbye. Tom couldn't think of any excuse for the hearse to avoid the Red Road – not now it had been newly tarmacked.

"Fine. Can one of you wait with the hearse?"

"I'm not staying here!" Claire exclaimed, sounding outraged at the suggestion. "God knows what little thugs this expensive vehicle will attract!"

"Christ, Claire, the people around here aren't animals!" Tom snarled, his tones almost contradicting his words. "They're not going to steal from a hearse!" He sounded a lot more convinced of that fact than he felt, but he'd be damned if he'd admit that to his wife.

"Fine. You stay here, then," Claire said sulkily.

"There's another hearse at the parlour I can call to collect this," the driver said, tactfully echoing Tom's gesture by waving at the coffin. "But it doesn't have rear seats, just one passenger seat at the front. Do you have another car that can take the rest of you to the crematorium?"

Tom was just about to say he'd have to go to his parents' flat after all to phone round some friends to see if anyone was available to drive them, when Claire surprised him by saying, "Yes, our son and daughter will be here any minute. Danny can give us all a lift. Tom can wait and go with the other hearse."

"*What?*" Tom gasped. "What do you mean, 'Danny can give us a—'"

"Tom, don't start that again," Claire snapped. "This nonsense stops now. Danny picked up his car from the repair shop yesterday, but he parked it at Kenny's house up the road because he didn't want you making a fuss about it. I said he and Hannah could have the afternoon off school to come to the funeral. They know Mrs Henderson was an old family friend of yours, and they wanted to pay their respects. It's just as well I did, isn't it? Else your parents would miss the funeral. The bus service around here is practically non-existent. Let's go."

She turned on her heel and marched away down the road towards the blocks of flats. The hearse driver followed her, keen to escape from the drama. Funerals were fraught enough at the best of times with all that sobbing and wailing. He didn't want to get caught in the middle of a shouting match.

But Tom didn't have any fight left in him. He slumped back against the hearse, feeling unsteady on his feet. A sense of foreboding had been building in his chest all week, and now his heart felt as though it was caught in a vice that was squeezing the life out of it. The thought of his children driving down the Red Road in a red Ford Escort, past the very spot he'd murdered his closest friends twenty-five years ago, was so terrifying he could barely breathe.

You have to stop them! he told himself. *It's you who deserves to be punished, not them. You're their father, for God's sake*! *Do something*!

The primal instinct of parenthood was what finally roused Tom from his stupor. He could run to the top of the road and wait for the red car. He could stop Danny and Hannah from turning off the main road. They could wait up there while he fetched Claire and his parents. They didn't need to drive down this road after all.

It was all going to be OK. He was thinking clearly now despite the distracting radio music that had grown from a soft whisper to a blaring noise in his ears.

Wait... What radio?

Tom turned to look through the hearse windows. There was no radio set in the dashboard. But the music was crystal clear, the words of the familiar song filling his head.

'We were only seventeen –
You were sweet and I was mean.
I got lost and then I found
Too late –
Emptiness without you around.'

Tom clamped his hands over his ears, but it didn't help. The words were louder than ever, repeating over and over as though the old record needle was jerking back to play the chorus again and again.

Ignore it! Tom's primal parental instinct was screaming at him. *Get to the top of the road and stop Danny's car*!

Tom listened to that voice instead. He was just turning away from the hearse to head up the road, when he saw something moving in the back. He stopped dead. The lid of the coffin was trembling, reacting to the thumping bass of the music that seemed to be sinking lower and lower in pitch until each beat felt like a mini earthquake. The flower bouquets shook violently, sliding to the floor as the coffin lid began to rise.

Tom stood transfixed in horror by the sight of the body within.

Mrs Henderson lay on her back in her best church dress and fake pearl necklace, the cream of her jacket contrasting sharply with the lurid red of crushed-velvet lining. Tom had spent hours choosing a soft padding that would look classy and reflect the expense he was going to, but instead the coffin lining gave the impression that the old woman was lying in a bath of blood.

What was worse, was that Mrs Henderson's head lay on one side, her face towards him and her open eyes staring at him accusingly. She'd heard him confess to killing her son. She'd never find peace from her sorrow in death, not now.

Tom backed away slowly.

She's dead she's dead she's dead, he told himself, forcing himself to turn away from those awful, accusing eyes.

But there was no let-up from the horrors to be found on the other side of the road. Chris and Jasmine stood on the pavement, the outline of their figures oddly blurred and translucent. In the sunlight, Tom could see every detail he'd missed on that dark night when his jealousy had blinded him. He saw the tears in Chris's eyes as he confessed his secret to Jasmine. He saw the sympathy in her beautiful green eyes as understanding dawned. She saw the way she put her arms around Chris – not, as he had supposed, as a lover, but as a friend comforting someone who was hurting.

That was the point he had driven down the Red Road that night and seen them, interpreting events through a fog of jealousy. He could hear the engine of his car revving as it sped down the hill towards him. He turned, resigned now to his fate, resigned to the just and fitting punishment that awaited him.

But when he looked round, he didn't see a ghost of his former self driving down the Red Road. The Ford Escort roaring down the road was real, his son behind the wheel and his daughter in the passenger seat. Hannah's eyes were wide with terror and Danny was waving at him, motioning wildly to his father to get off the road. The car was coming at him faster and faster, and Tom gasped when he realised why.

He'd cut every wire he could reach in that car's engine, including the brake cable. He hadn't cared what repair shop Danny took it to – Tom had assumed the car would be written off. No reputable mechanic would touch the mess he'd made of it. None except the Pikeman brothers. After they'd given up burglary years ago, they'd set themselves up with a garage business at the edge of town. Gavin and Ryan Pikeman were cut-price con men, and if Danny had taken his car to them, then they would have done their usual bare-minimum fix-up for cash-in-hand, no questions asked. They wouldn't be particular about replacing brake cables with new ones, they'd just patch up the old ones. You got what you paid for with the Pikeman brothers, and after buying a car on his part-time, minimum-wage salary, Danny couldn't pay for squat.

His brake cable had given out at the first hill he'd encountered. The long hill of the Red Road.

Tom's mind raced as he watched the car speed towards him, trying to work out if the forecourt between the buildings would be wide enough for Danny to drive around and lose momentum before he hit something. Yes, he decided, as long as Danny kept on going down the hill, as long as no one got in the way of the car, then his kids could ride it out until the car lost speed on the flat.

With the hearse taking up one lane of the road, Tom needed to get out of the way fast. He stepped onto the pavement…

…and promptly fell sprawling back onto the road. Something had blocked his way, pushing him with malign force into the path of the speeding car.

Tom looked up to see the two ghostly figures glaring down at him from the edge of the pavement. Chris's eyes were glowing red, while Jasmine's were a blazing green. They'd waited twenty-five years for revenge. Today it would be his blood that painted the Red Road, his flesh ground like minced beef into the concrete.

Tom threw a hand over his head as the red Ford Escort bore down on him, just the way Chris and Jasmine had done when he'd driven full speed at them. His body tensed, but the blow didn't come.

Instead, there was the sound of screaming, the roar of an engine, then a crash so loud it was ear splitting.

"No...!" Tom groaned as he rolled over on the road. Danny had jerked the wheel at the last second rather than run over his father. The Ford Escort had crashed full speed into the back of the hearse, metal slamming into metal, shredding flesh and bone on impact.

The flesh and bone of his children.

Tom staggered to his feet, wailing aloud when he saw what was left of his son and daughter through the shattered windscreen and twisted wreckage. All the colour in his world disappeared, blurring into vivid red, then fading to deathly grey. Sounds grew muffled – the hissing of the crumpled engine, the ghostly radio music from the hearse and the whispering voice that Tom only realised was repeating the words of the prophetic poem in his ear when the last lines finally faded away to silence.

'War declared and a grave prepared,

A sudden blow and blood did flow
Down the red, red road.'

Twenty-five years after Tom had ground his best friend and girlfriend into the Red Road, blood flowed from the mangled bodies of his children and dripped onto the concrete, forming little rivers that pooled around Tom's feet. Tom stared at it in horrified fascination before turning to plead with the two spectres on the pavement to undo what they'd done and bring his children back. But Chris and Jasmine were gone. He was alone on the Red Road, alone with two corpses representing the ruin of all his hopes and dreams.

No, *three* corpses.

Tom's glassy eyes sought out the open coffin that had been concertinaed between the rear door of the hearse and the back of the rear seats. He expected to see a pulped corpse tangled in the remains of shattered wood. But the rear doors crashing against the coffin had hit Mrs Henderson feet-first, pushing the dead woman into a sitting position, her corpse now propped up against the back of the passenger seats. Her head was resting on her chest, her eyes now closed, and the lips that before were fixed in a grimace of shock, now wore the hint of a gentle smile.

Tom had paid for his terrible crimes at last.

The old woman was finally at peace.

About the author

Victoria Williamson is an award-winning author from Glasgow, Scotland who has worked as an educator in a number of different countries, including as an English teacher in China, a secondary school science teacher in Cameroon, a teacher trainer in Malawi, and an additional support needs teacher in the UK.

Victoria works part time writing books for the education company Twinkl and spends the rest of her time writing novels for children and adults, and visiting schools, libraries and literary festivals to give author talks and run creative writing workshops. When not writing or talking about books, she's often to be found up to her knees in mud on an archaeological dig or tangled up in a ball of wool playing with a crochet hook.

Her favourite time of year is autumn, when mists descend on the Scottish moors and eerie stories like the tales in *Tainted Towns* come whispering on the wind on twilight evenings.

Website: www.strangelymagical.com

X @strangelymagic

@strangelmagicalbooks

If you enjoyed *Tainted Towns*, why not try:

Five unnerving tales of the weird and uncanny from award-winning author Victoria Williamson.
Out now with Silver Thistle Press

A room full of screaming butterflies.
An unsettling smile on the face of a carved sarcophagus.
A painting that draws its viewer into the disturbing past.
A stuffed bear that growls in the dead of night.
And a shell that whispers more sinister sounds than the sigh of the sea…

Dare you cross the threshold of the old Museum and view its eerie exhibits?

Printed in Great Britain
by Amazon

63161406R00122